Immortal L.A.

Christina / Boss Woman

Thank you so much for coming out and seeing us. Listen to my brother he is smarter than he looks.

Eric Czuleger

Love
Eric
4-21-18

Copyright © Eric Czuleger 2014

All rights reserved

License Notes

All rights reserved. This book is licensed for your personal enjoyment only. This book may not be re-sold or given away to other people. If you would like to share this book with another person, please purchase an additional copy for each person. If you are reading this book and did not purchase it, or it was not purchased for your use only, then please return to the vendor and purchase your own copy. Thank you for respecting the hard work of this author.

For my Mom

For my Brother

For my Dad

Contents

L.A. History 1 1

The Meeting 9

Open on Angel 22

L.A. History 2 60

Punksnotdead.. 66

L.A. History 3 96

The Vampire Andy 103

L.A. History 4 125

Wolf Skin 131

Mastermind..160

Satan Gets a Facelift 187

L.A. History 5 202

Coming soon... 207

Acknowledgements 223

About the Author...225

The San Andreas Fault is the gateway to hell. The Hollywood Hills are mass graves of angels. William Mulholland defies God himself. Satan gets plastic surgery on Sunset Boulevard. A dead boy is stuck in traffic next to a vampire who can't sleep, and an angel who has a an audition for the role of an angel. The stars are in the sky and on the pavement. The wolves are prowling. The weather is perfect. The screenplay is written. The soul is sold. This movie is going to be big- really big. Welcome to Immortal L.A. You're going to love it here.

"Los Angeles give me some of you! Los Angeles come to me the way I came to you, my feet over your streets, you pretty town I loved you so much, you sad flower in the sand, you pretty town."

   -John Fante
      Ask the Dust

*It's the edge of the world
And all of western civilization
The sun may rise in the East
At least it's settled in a final location
It's understood that Hollywood sells Californication*

*Pay your surgeon very well
To break the spell of ageing
Celebrity skin, is this your chin
Or is it war your waging?*

   -Red Hot Chili Peppers
      Californication

*California... knows how to party
California... knows how to party
In the citaaaaay of L.A.*

   -Tupac Shakur (Feat. Dr. Dre)
      California Love

.

L.A. History 1

The Abridged Corrected History of Los Angeles
"Battlefield of Angels"
10,298 B.C.-1790 A.D.

The city of Los Angeles is the most populous and diverse in the state of California. It is the second most populous in the United States. Current census data estimates a population of around 3,800,000 human residents. The city's historically rich tradition is largely due to its ethnically diverse population and geographic position. It is situated on the coastline of the Pacific Ocean and rests on the tectonically active San Andreas Fault. This fault line is a meeting point of the Pacific and the American Tectonic plates. The San Andreas Fault is also a well-known doorway to Hell and an ancient terrestrial battlefield littered with the bodies of angels. This accounts for Los Angeles hosting the largest population of supernatural, omni-natural, unnatural, and pseudonatural beings and quasi-beings in the continental United States. It also accounts for the La Brea Tar Pits.

Filipe de Neve officially founded Los Angeles in 1781. However, the ancient texts of lost Apocrypha guarded by the undying Knights Templar in the secret library of Los Angeles under Pershing Square, clearly states otherwise. The rich history of Los Angeles begins long before the first human beings ever set foot on the semi-arid soil.

Evidence revealed in Dr. Daniel Crutchin's ground breaking thesis "On the Existence and Preponderance of Indigenous Supernatural Creatures in Mezzo-America," states that the indigenous human population of the Los Angeles River Basin were, more than likely, fallen angels exiled in the Great Angel Uprising of 10,298 B.C.E. It was this same uprising wherein Lucifer, conductor of the choirs of angels was cast out of heaven by a vengeful God. Rebellious angels led by Lucifer clashed with angels loyal to God in the area that is now known as West Hollywood.

It's common knowledge that angels grossify considerably during the process of terrestrial integration. Though they lose much of their previous form they do retain distant memories of their celestial past. This accounts for the rich spiritual lives and celestial powers of early Californians. This also accounts for their battlefield prowess and superior rug making skills.

Second First Contact

In 1542 the Portuguese adventurer Juan Rodriguez Cabrillo explored the California coast at the behest of Spanish King Philip II. Upon seeing modern San Pedro Bay he dubbed it *Baya De Los Fumos* or the "Bay of Smokes". Fringe historians claim this was due to an early winter fog on the bay, or perhaps smoke blowing in from aboriginal campfires. However, mainstream sources understand that the sea was, in fact, boiling from The Great and Terrible Sea Monster living at the bottom of the Redondo Beach Trench. Off the coast of modern day Redondo Beach is a subducted ocean trench that forms the cleavage joint between the Pacific Plate and American Plate. Cabrillo was able to safely steer his ship, *The San Salvador*, to dock in the modern era Bay of Santa Monica. Had he not, he would have been kept forever in undying purgatory at the bottom of the ocean to keep The Great and Terrible Sea Monster company. The Great and Terrible Sea Monster off the Southern California coast takes to fits of melancholy and often seeks the company of the half living.

It should be noted that fog off of the coast of Southern California is actually quite rare. The weather is always perfect. Always. This is due partially to the off shore coastal breeze and the Jetstream down the coast from Oregon. Mostly, it is because of the tribal dances and human sacrifices of the mezzo-American Indians (read: angels grossified). In the words of historian Dr. Daniel Crutchin,

"The tribal leaders attempted to recreate the weather of heaven on earth. They bargained for a maximum of 10 days of rain a year and a week of clouds. Many human beings were sacrificed to reach this deal. The loss of life is largely understood to have been worth it. Nothing beats a beautiful day in Los Angeles. Nothing."

The natives killed Cabrillo while he attempted to save his men from being sacrificed to The Great and Terrible Sea Monster in order to reduce the amount of cloudy days a year to only three. The men planned to continue their expedition, when an earthquake opened a great rift into the heart of the inferno. Upon viewing the infernal majesty of Hell, the men decided that he had discovered enough for one expedition, and that Cabrillo would have wanted them to return home. The *San Salvador* sailed back to Spain by Cabrillo's second in command who related the information to King Phillip II that the new world was, in fact, a doorway to Hell. It was recommended that further expeditions include a garrison of warrior priests and demon hunters. It was added in the report that the weather was incredibly pleasant. Philip II, influenced by the growing Age of Enlightenment in Europe, dismissed these claims as superstition and far too much time spent on a boat.

In 1755 The Great Lisbon Earthquake leveled large sections of Portugal and Spain. The great earthquake inspired Voltaire's famous verses, *Poem Sur le Desastre de Lisbonne*. It also inspired Philip II's fear of God once more. He set about requisitioning, recruiting, and training a garrison of demon hunting warrior priests from The Vatican. The garrison sought to seal up the gateway to hell by constructing a series of twenty-one missions along the California coast. They were also tasked with the introduction of European staple crops and the conversion of native peoples to Catholicism.

The Warrior Monks of California

The highest ranking amongst the warrior-monks was Father Junipero Serra. Originally, Miguel Joseph Serra, he took the name Junipero after Saint Juniper. He was renown amongst the Franciscans for his philosophical insight, extreme devotion, and marksmanship. He left Spain at the age of 27 to serve as superior to the group of fifteen Franciscan warrior-monks. While typical Franciscans tie their habit with a chord knotted three times to symbolize poverty, chastity, and obedience, these Franscians added an additional two knots for deadliness and carnage. To aid in his journey to The New World, Pope Clement XIII famously gave Fr. Serra a set of blessed Lorinzoni Flintlock pistols, a swatch of the Shroud of Turin, and immortality.

Serra oversaw the development and construction of the twenty-one missions. He slayed hundreds of demons and confirmed over 5,000 new Catholics. As a footnote to Serra's corpse-littered past, he also famously donated almost one-hundred-and-forty dollars to George Washington to aid in the American Revolution. It would not take him long to realize the horrible mistake that he had made. Father Junipero Serra currently works at a Hollywood discount movie theatre. An unfortunate demon attack left him unable to speak without aid by an electronic voice box. He regrets his immortality daily.

The Elder Angels

It is important to note the role of the Tongva Indians in the development of early Los Angeles. Had it not been for their intervention in the late 1770s modern day Los Angeles would be a metropolitan capital in Hell. The earliest Spanish settlements in the modern day Los Angeles River Basin would become the site of a massive battle between angels and demons. Roused to action by the staunchly Catholic settlers along the San Andreas Fault, Hell gaped wide and vomited its spawn onto the earth to claim the souls of the living. Heaven responded accordingly, unleashing celestial phalanxes of angels to battle the encroaching darkness. The Spanish settlers hastily loaded flintlock rifles and draped themselves in rosary beads to prepare for the battle.

The Diary of Padre Fernando Vargas was uncovered in the 1960s clutched in the hands of his preserved body dredged from the La Brea Tar Pits. It remains the finest primary source available on the 1771 First Battle of Heaven and Hell, as it would come to be known. Vargas writes:

> *The Angels have adorned themselves with war-like wings of iron, gold, and platinum. The Others (read: Demons) let out unholy cries from between dagger-like teeth. They run, gnashing and tearing like madmen, at the white robed angels. A kind of ecstatic joy comes to them as they tear the tongues and eyes from the angels. From my chamber I can see that a malignant cloud reeking of decay and blood has formed in the sky above the pueblo. In the floodplain below is a graveyard of broken beautiful bodies. I confess now that my faith will go to the victor. I will kneel down and call Satan "God" if only to be spared the pit from which these creatures come.*

A replica of Vargas's body is on display at the Page Museum on Wilshire Boulevard on the second floor, between the Woolly Mammoth and the Men's Restroom. The real body is in the museum basement. Waiting.

The Living Goddess

The tide of the battle turned when Archangel Gabriel descended to lead a final offensive against the encroaching demons. The Spanish were unable to repel the attacks given their devout belief in the power of Satan. In a brilliant tactical maneuver Gabriel enlisted the help of the native Tongva people. The Tongva Indians were religiously animist and did not believe in Satan or demons. Satan was powerless against the elder gods and lesser deities of the Tongva.

The Angel Gabriel led them into battle against the demons. The Tongva used their native magicks and healing herbs to aid the angels in their final offensive. The last garrison of demons were pinned down in the Caheunga Pass and annihilated by a hail of arrows and spears. The Tongva saved the Los Angeles river basin from being swallowed up by the earth and becoming a part of the unholy inferno. The Spanish Settlers were grateful though not entirely impressed. As a measure of their gratitude, the settlers gave the natives rosaries.

The bodies of the angels were piled upon one another and covered with earth. The mass graves have come to form what we now know as the Hollywood Hills. The demon bodies were tossed into the river of Los Angeles. They promptly turned to gold, as all demon bodies do when they touch water.

The indigenous peoples were so grateful to the Archangel Gabriel that they took on the Spanish pseudonym, *Los Gabrilenos*. The Spanish missionaries were so grateful they continued their efforts to convert the indigenous people to Catholicism. However, by 1787 the Tongva had grown weary of the constant Spanish intrusion into their territory. They turned to 9-year-old Toypurina, a Tongva medicine woman believed to be a living goddess. She unified the indigenous tribes and mobilized four of the surrounding villages into an assault on the Spanish Pueblo.

Pablo Cota, Sargent of the Spanish army stationed in the burgeoning Pueblo of Los Angeles wrote in his 1788 letter to a garrison stationed in Navidad, Mexico:

The pagans set upon us in the form of wild things. They used their magicks to confuse our men and set them shooting wildly. They attacked in the forms of wolves, bears, and bobcats. When at long last we apprehended their leader, we found her to be a nine-year-old girl, strong in the pagan arts. A truce was agreed to if we would call her The Queen of the Angels. We have henceforth renamed the Pueblo, El Pueblo Nuestra Senora la Reina de los Angeles de Porciuncula (The Town of Our Lady of the Queen of the Angels of the River Porciuncula). Governor Philipe De Neve has made the requisite changes to all official documents in order to avoid a curse.

Toypurina was weary from resistance at the age of 14, considered to be very old for a medicine woman. Eventually she succumbed entirely to The Spanish intrusion. She converted to Catholicism, and changed her name to Regina Josepha. She died in 1799. Even today she is widely regarded as the Queen of the Angels both living and dead. The name *El Pueblo Nuestra Senora La Reina de Los Angeles de Porciuncula* was later shortened to Los Angeles. In common parlance it is referred to as L.A.

The strange and wonderful history of Los Angeles becomes only more strange and wonderful as it progresses into the 1800s. Heaven and Hell, as we will see, are known to make their desires understood in peculiar and horrific ways. This is especially true in the portion of Los Angeles known as Hollywood.

The Meeting

His fingernails are clean. His belt buckle is silver. You can see the ceiling in the toes of his shoes. He speaks in a silken baritone.

"My question is this: Are you using it for anything?

Because if you're NOT using it for anything, why have it? You know what I mean?

"I had a- you know? A Bowflex once. You know the Bowflex, right? Yeah, the Bowflex. It's a workout machine. I was going to get in the best shape of my life. I don't really NEED to work out, but I thought I would see what the fuss was about.

I ordered the thing off of the TV because IN THOSE DAYS-

In those days- you could order stuff off of the TV.

"I'm old. I get it, but I don't look a day over 30 right?

I know what the answer is 'no' so don't bother being polite.

I was around in the days when you ordered from the Sears and Roebucks catalogue! I was around in the days when you went to a blacksmith. I was around in the days when you snuck up on another person in the forest and tried to break their head with a rock so you could take their food.

"I'm old.

"Online stuff is new to me, but it's good. I'm adjusting, that's the secret to longevity in this business or any other. Always adjust. Oh, so the Bowflex! I get the thing. I don't know how to put it together. I don't know how to use it. The instructions didn't even come with it. So, what does it do? It sits in its box. It collects dusts. It's not helping anyone and no one is helping it. It may as well not be there. If a friend came by and said, 'Oh hey, a Bowflex.' I would say:

"Yeah! Do you want it? I'm not using it."

"I'm a good friend. I'm a good friend with some useless crap that I'm not using. First and foremost though: I'm a good friend.

I'm not saying that it's useless crap. I'm just asking you... Are you using it?"

Rachel shifts in her chair. The chair is rich, expensive leather. She wants to be wrapped in it for winter hibernation. It sits across from an enormous mahogany desk. This is the only office on the top floor of a completely empty building at the corner of Francisco and 7th street in Downtown Los Angeles. It is the kind of building that you dismiss as another honeycomb of corporate workspaces or multi-national bank offices, populated by the faceless yet well dressed.

If you have the time to watch and wait you will see that no one ever enters that building except for the occasional homeless man looking for a place to use the restroom. You will see a blonde secretary at the front desk. You will see a security guard with a baton and a handgun. The secretary is smiling, the security guard is not. They are both waiting, watching. If you go at any hour of the day or the night you will see them: waiting, watching. But you won't notice this, because you are too busy doing other things. There is only one security

IMMORTAL L.A.

guard and one secretary because there is only one office. All of the other floors are completely empty. Steel support columns, concrete, and whistling wind.

Rachel sits in his office. He waits for her answer. There are no walls. Only windows. The skyline of Los Angeles encircles a desk and a chair. An elevator bank and a washroom spring up from the floor. Interior architecture of the infamous and infinite. He is the most important person in Los Angeles and he knows it. This makes him the 14th most important person in the world, though he thinks he is the 4th.

He sits on his desk. His feet do not touch the ground, because of its size. He kicks his feet back and forth like a child. He is never still. He moves like a dancer, like a cat. He is coiled energy ready to spring. His reputation precedes him like a freight train.

"Are you using it?" he asks again, smile broadening like melting butter.

Rachel considers her answer to his question and adjusts in the leather chair. She wears her best clothes, a red pencil skirt, white blouse, and a red Prada jacket that she plans on returning immediately after this meeting. She cannot afford this jacket. When she got an invitation to this building she immediately vomited and then went on a juice fast. She used a teeth-whitening kit three times, she hit her yoga class twice a day and began going to bed at 9 P.M. when her schedule permitted. Which was never. She is hungry, and tired, and minty, and flexible and shiny, and she looks wonderful. She feels like a hollow cathedral. She does not know the answer to the question. He doesn't mind.

He hops off his desk, and his shoes *clack* on the black marble floor. He sucks air in through his teeth and rubs his pure white hands together in slow concentric circles.

"Don't answer yet. I'm not a namedropper. I don't need to impress anyone. You know about me because you know about me.

You probably have some idea of who I am and what I do. No one can drop my name because no one knows my name. That's a valuable asset. This is all about developing assets. I want you to be an asset to me. I could tell you a long list of names of people who are assets to me. These are people who do good, wonderful, things in the world for you and me and starving children and everyone. They're able to change the world for the better because they have come into my unique fold.

This, like so many offers, is only a one-time thing.

I'm sorry to say that, but it is the case. I need a producer for this project, and it needs to be someone I have on the team. It has been handed to me personally by... Well, let's say the team captain. I want you on my team. So, what do you say Rachel?"

Rachel feels like she is breathing either too quickly or too slowly, she cannot tell which. Her calf is shaking and she is trying to silence the rhythmic *tap-tap-tap* of her heel on the marble. She speaks.

"I think I use my soul." Silence, except for the *tap-tap-tap*. He smiles.

"And, I'm... If this... If what you're saying... if this is a real thing..." Rachel leans forward and raises her eyebrows, giving him a chance to announce that this is all an overdramatic test of ethics. He leans forward and raises his perfectly manicured eyebrows. He says nothing.

"I... I try to be a good person," Rachel continues. "I try.

And I *use* my soul."

The word *try* echoes in her head like a scream in a cave.

She just told a lie. She knows that she shouldn't lie. The room feels wrong because nothing feels wrong about it. A leather strap is pulling tight deep in her gut. She is promising herself bed, Xanax, and celebrity news if she can make it out of this office without falling to pieces.

He runs a hand across his face and up the back of his neck. He smiles like a sunbeam coming through an open window, gently warming a piece of carpet that a cat is napping on. He leans casually on his desk.

"See, that's not your fault. That's the culture. That's just THIS culture. You're mistaking religion for business.

You're mistaking belief for ethics. You've got it all mixed up!

Here, in this place, and this time, it's all divided. But *business* is different. We're talking *business* here.

You have something that I would like to trade you for.

I will trade you astronomic success for your soul. Simple simple. No monsters, no saints, no big bad wolves, no ulterior motives. I get something, you get something, and we all get a movie.

"Is it a cliché? Yes. I'm aware of that. Do clichés come from somewhere? Duh. Do I have this exact conversation every single time I meet with someone here? Oh, you bet. I'm not going to say names, but there is a reason that these windows don't open any more. We've had some *things* happen. But I know who to bring up here and who to leave down there.

"I know that you're a climber. I hear things. I see things. Your name comes up in certain circles. I invite you to my office. And here. We. Are. Get good and bad out of your head. If you're thinking good and bad, you're not going to get anywhere here. We're just talking about two sides of the same coin. We're talking about THE MOVIES gosh darnit!

"It's all make believe."

He walks around his desk. He picks a screenplay and he drops it on his desk with a loud *slap!* He looks at her. He jumps up on the desk and kicks his legs back and forth. He picks up the screenplay and flips through the pages.

"What... What is that?" Rachel asks.

He tosses the script across to her and it lands perfectly in her lap. It reads *Untitled*.

"Is it good?" She levels her eyes toward him. A smile splashes on his face and she wants to perish in it. She puts out the flame. She needs to negotiate. She knows how to negotiate. He clears his throat.

"Honestly, no. It's not great. It's not so much that it's BAD, it's just been done about a billion times. But it's the movies! We reinvent the wheel every day; we just package it in different ways. It's exactly the kind of thing WE like. It's the kind of thing the interested parties I represent appreciate. It's vampires, and angels, and permissible teen eroticism under the guise of fantasy. Fun, fun, fun stuff. Harmless. The good thing is; we get everybody into the theatre. Tweens, teens, inbetweeners, millenials, twentysomethings, flirty-thirties, DIRTY-thirties, and of course the forgotten forties, everyone else will be dragged by someone they know.

"Blockbuster material here. People wait their whole lives for a stack of pages just like that."

Rachel suddenly has to pee. She squeezes her knees together and riffles the pages. Words, phrases, character names, screen directions, jump out at her, meaningless without context. Doesn't matter. If he says it's a winner it is a winner. She runs a tongue along her slick white teeth. She squeezes her knees together tighter. She wonders what her family in Fairfield, Iowa would say about this if she told them. They're transcendental meditators and Olympian relativists. They share the convenient dinner-party acceptable beliefs of the economically fortunate. God is a difficult word problem that isn't on their test. She would not tell them. She couldn't tell them. They would not recognize her in her jacket.

She feels her heart beating in her chest beneath her Prada jacket. With each beat she had to pee more. She wonders if her soul is somewhere between her heart and her bladder. She imagines it like a blue mist with a soft light at its core. It emits a gentle warmth, and it helps her discern right from wrong. It tells her what music she loves. It smells like the melting sugar on the top of a crème brule. It grows brighter when she holds her dog to her chest. She can't afford her dog, but she loves him. She wonders what it would be like to just have a heart in her chest with no soul to accompany it. What would it be like to feel your heart beating and nothing else?

"I just need a producer. And I need a producer that no one knows. We like to promote from the very bottom. We're in the business of making dreams come true after all."

He smiles. It is the smile from an advertisement for men's watches. It is a smile like a good armchair. It is a smile that would make babies have sweet dreams and old women wink at one another. She crosses her knees and bites her bottom lip.

Rachel produces independent horror films and public service announcements about the dangers of huffing paint thinner. She takes jobs that are jobs. She takes as many jobs as she can. She crushes her personal life under the heel of the boots she cannot afford. She will have love and friendship and late night talks over cheap bottles of wine with people who she can share secrets with. She will have these things when she can afford them. She pushes and pushes against this city forgoing everything for the opportunity to afford stillness.

The screenplay is heavy, thick white paper. It feels good in her hands. She crosses her knees tighter and digs her nails into the paper. She wants it. She doesn't care what is in the pages. She wants it. She goes for the kill.

"Fine. I know who you are. I know the reputation that you have. I would be an idiot to not take this project. And if you know about me, you know I am not dumb." Rachel uncrosses her legs.

"So, why do you want my soul?" She raises her eyebrow.

"I want it because I want it." He runs two fingers down the sides of his silk tie, smoothing unseen wrinkles.

"That's not good enough." He stops smiling. She takes a deep breath and continues.

"You don't just invite anyone up here and I'm here. I bet that it's a little bit harder than just finding anyone to produce a movie. You can't swing a cat without hitting someone who calls themselves a producer around here. So, what do you want MY soul for?

"I don't really believe in all of that, so it's meaningless to me. I'll give you my soul like my business card. Except my business card is worth more. I buy the expensive card stock." That is another lie, her business cards are cheap and flimsy, but she needs some wiggle room.

"As far as I'm concerned, you're an eccentric money guy who has a good track record for picking winners. I want a winner. I want to be an asset for you. But if I'm indulging you by claiming that I've got a soul, and that I can give it to you, you have to meet me half way. What do you want to do with my particular soul?" She felt like she was going to explode, but she couldn't excuse herself to the restroom, it would show weakness, it would be a retreat.

He walks slowly around his desk. One. Step. At. A. Time. He sits down and kicks his feet onto the corner of the desk. He looks at her. His face is blank. He places his fingertips together under his nose.

"I've never talked to someone about the logistics of what I do before. This is interesting."

Rachel grinds her teeth together and levels her eyes at him. Rachel is going to die if she cannot relieve herself. "Cards on the table. I'm a collector and an advertiser. A brand manager really. People in my position exist in, let's say, areas of influence. I am trying to get a point of view across.

I am trying to promote my employer's brand. What my employer cares about is what any employer cares about. They want their numbers up and their brand recognizable. I make that happen, and I have incredible resources. However, I need to make sure that any candidates are on the level. I need a commitment.

"Some people are Pepsi people, some people are Coke people.

Let's just say, I want everyone to be a Pepsi person. Two sides of the same coin. That script has a lot of product placement in it. Do you take my meaning?"

Rachel shifts in her seat. She fantasizes about knocking the chair over and hurling herself towards the restroom. Then she sees it. She sees a bit of sadness float past his eyes. She has a foothold. She steadies her voice.

"Am I to understand that you are an asset of your employer? You gave away your soul, too?" He looks out the windows at an uncharacteristically dark cloud moving across the Hollywood hills. He nods his head. A smile crosses his lips and then passes.

"Do you miss it?"

He takes a deep breath in and lets it out slowly.

"I don't remember what it was like to have it. But, yes, sometimes I think I do miss it. Sometimes. It's been a long time. It's fine though. I'm great. I'm fine." He looks to Rachel and places his hands on his desk, spreading them wide in front of him.

"Was it worth it?"

He nods his head. Slow, measured, absolutely sure.

"You love what you love in the world. You do whatever you can to keep doing it. I love the movies. I always have, and I always will. I have a very clear understanding of what *always* means. I know you love the movies too. So yes, it was worth it. I get to make those lights happen on that screen. If I had to explain to you why that is important, you wouldn't be here."

An arrow sinks deep into her heart. A chill runs down the back of her neck. The warm blue cloud in her chest pulses brightly, her heart beats.

"Okay. I'll do it. I'll give you my soul."

He looks at her. He does not smile.

"You don't believe in it anyway do you?"

"No." She hears the word coming out of her mouth.

"Good. It's better that way." He opens the top drawer of his desk and takes out a contract.

"Do I sign it in blood?" She stands up and moves to the desk, trying to walk as normally as possible. She would sell her soul twice over to run to the bathroom.

"A pen will work. Blood is very difficult to write with. Some people stick to the old ways. We're oddballs. Our office is trying to become entirely paperless to reduce our carbon footprint. This has to be signed in person. Honestly, it makes no sense to use as much paper as some of the other offices do. Just sign there."

He points to a line with an X on it. The entire contract reads, *I promise my soul to* _____

"Why isn't the name filled in?"

"We fill it in later. Let's just assume that you're promising your soul to Pepsi." He hands her a heavy silver pen. It feels cool and beautiful in her fingers. Her hand signs the document before she realizes what she is doing. She gives the pen back. He places his hands around hers. They feel warm and strong. He curls her fingers around the pen.

"Keep it. You'll want it. I still have mine."

"Thanks. Can I use your restroom?"

"Yeah, right back there by the elevator."

Rachel tries not to run to the restroom. The marble floor makes her nervous in her heels. She throws herself into the bathroom and slams the door behind her. She wriggles free of her skirt, and her Spanx and forgoes the layer of protective paper between her and the seat. She relieves herself with eye-rolling intensity.

She gets up and begins strapping herself back into her armor. She catches sight of herself in the mirror. She undoes the buttons on her blouse and leaves her skirt around her knees. She is ribs and abs, with pale skin pulled tight. She can see the crow's feet and laugh lines blossoming on her face. She sees everywhere she is hard where she should be soft, wrinkled where she should be smooth, and fleshy where there should be muscle.

She looks into her eyes. She cannot tell if there is a soul missing from where it should be. She smiles. White, straight, clear as the beach after a good rain. Those whitening kits must have worked. She washes and dries her hands under the blow drier. She doesn't look at herself as she leaves.

Rachel carries the screenplay under her arm. She walks two blocks up 7th street to the parking lot where she left her Prius so no one would see it. The screenplay rides shotgun. She thinks about buckling it into the seat. She plays no music in the car. She listens to no NPR. She feels like the sound that an empty water tower makes when you hit it with a shovel. She looks at her cellphone; she wants to call someone and tell them everything. She realizes that she doesn't have anyone to tell even if she could tell them. She is hungry, but she wants nothing to do with the vanilla Powerbars and coconut water she keeps in her glove compartment. She picks up a burrito and a bottle of wine. It's dark out when she falls into her apartment.

Her dog stands smiling next to a pool of its urine. Its small pink tongue pokes out with every huffing breath. Rachel leaves her burrito, bottle of wine, and screenplay on an upturned moving box. She has lived in this apartment for nine months. She keeps meaning to throw the box out and get a real side table. She cleans up the pee with headshots from a long past audition. Her dog jumps onto its hind legs and paws at the air. It spins in circles for her. She scratches the roll of fat at the back of its neck with her manicured nails. She strips herself out of her clothes. She lays the Prada jacket on her bed so that she can return it in the morning. She washes her makeup off, puts her glasses on, and jumps into sweats and a t-shirt.

She watches *The Actual Persian Housewives of Los Angeles*. She drinks wine. She eats her burrito. Her dog watches her. She pats the space next to her on the couch. The dog hops up with a little bit of help. It headbutts her ribs playfully. She puts her arm around the dog. She squeezes. She feels her heart beat. It licks her cheek. She feels her heart beat. She holds it out in front of her and looks in its big dumb eyes. She feels her heart beat.

She turns the television off. She puts her burrito down. She picks up *Untitled*. She turns the first page. She feels her heart beat harder.

The opening screen directions read: *We open on Angel.*

Open on Angel

1

The Angel looked at her headshots. The 8X10 matte picture smiled at her. She smiled back at the photo. She tilted her head up and smiled at the rest of the women in the waiting room. All of them were blonde, like The Angel. All of them beautiful like The Angel. They, for all intents and purposes, looked like angels. Of course none of them were angels. The thought then crossed her mind that she wasn't an angel any more either. The thought rose a rustle of despair in her heart, and then utter excitement that she had felt despair. A giggle jumped out of her mouth breaking the silence in the room. Fourteen blonde heads turned to the giggling fallen Angel. She smiled broadly.

"I'm excited!" she proclaimed to the fourteen women and the water dispenser in the corner of the room. They responded with blank stares, and a not-so-whispered *crazy bitch*. The Angel kept smiling. None of the women in the room smiled back at The Angel. Some stared at their headshots. Some mouthed lined from the scripts in front of them. Some stared into nothingness and breathed deep, dull terror. The water machine *glug-glugged* in the corner. Everyone looked at it and then returned to their private galaxies. The Angel smiled. This was exactly what she wanted. If she had anyone to pray to in Heaven, she would have sent up a prayer of thanks.

The door of the audition room opened. The entire room snapped to attention. Hair tousled, legs uncrossed, backs straightened, and chests pushed forward. One woman let out a good-natured laugh as if responding to a joke that no one had told. The Angel smiled. Another blonde walked out of the audition room followed by a man resembling a turtle. She turned and mumbled *thank you for the opportunity*. He ignored her and buried his nose in a clipboard balanced against his stomach. "Jezebel Storm!" The turtle man said with a nasal whine. A tall blonde rose from her seat in the corner of the room.

Only one more until me, thought The Angel. As Jezebel Storm strode by, The Angel yelped, *"Good luck!"* first startling and then annoying all of the other blondes. They snuck looks at The Angel and then to one another. For a moment, all of the blondes were united in mutual disgust. This town will eat her alive, they thought, without realizing that she had already died. The Angel smiled to herself knowing full well the power of her good wishes to Ms. Storm. Across the room one of the blonde's eyes lingered on The Angel.

The Angel locked eyes with her and the woman quickly buried her face in her script. She was more homely than the rest. She knew it. She sat like she were born to be the least beautiful woman in the room. With her every breath she apologized for her existence.

She had big feet and a hawkish nose. She was caked in makeup, giving her the appearance of a slutty clown. She was crossing and uncrossing her legs while absentmindedly pinching at the hem of her top to make sure that it covered the small pink roll of fat, which crept out from the top of her jeans. Earthly problems were not something The Angel was accustomed to. She took the leap out of heaven on her own and she had catching up to do.

The Angel resented the term "falling from grace." It was less like falling and more like filling out the appropriate paperwork followed by turning it into your boss. Of course, the term boss isn't used in Heaven. They prefer *Eternal Work Coach*. The Angel resented that term too. But, resentment doesn't exist in Heaven either.

Her Eternal Work Coach was a gentle old seraphim who liked to recount stories about the old days when they formed flying phalanxes in the sky to fight demons. He was crisscrossed with scars from battles long past. If pressed, he would tell you that he preferred when time and space didn't exist and there was no paperwork. He was sad to see her go. When she turned in her form, he double stamped it, handed it back and held her hand between his two warm paws. She saw the unmistakable scar of demon teeth deep in his hand. She knew that her next life would contain a thousand more wounds.

"Just stay how you are and you come right back. Stay good. You come right back. You know the rules. Don't forget now, okay? I'll miss you around here." She thanked him and asked where the elevator was.

The water dispenser *glugged*. The Angel's eyes returned to the blonde on the other side of the room. She was knees and elbows, long limbs and big feet, wide shoulders and a small chest. Yet, there was something that made her shine.

That's when The Angel heard a prayer:

It was a slight whisper in the back room of her heart. It rang like golden bell tones, more music than language. *"Help me get this. Please. I know you're there."*

Since her incarnation, The Angel's ability to hear prayers was fading like the feeling from a phantom limb. Still, in close proximity, prayers rang loud and sweet like she was in the choir again. The Angel looked around the room trying to determine the source of the sound.

They were all gazing into the electric glow of their smart phones. The Angel's attention was drawn to the big-footed blonde across from her. Her head was slightly bowed, and the roll of fat had escaped from its hiding place. Her hands were not clasped but her lips were moving wordlessly. It was a prayer of necessity from the hopeless. It was the sweetest kind of prayer, the prayer of someone who has no recourse but to pray.

The Angel wanted to sing, but she couldn't. Music on earth wasn't like music in heaven. Heaven was made of music. It was a symmetrical mandala of golden choir stands with an empty space where the conductor once stood. The golden glowing rows repeated infinitely. They had always been and would always be. It smelled like warm rose water. She was nostalgic for her choir of cherubim. Each choir of angels intoned their set of prayers to the higher order. Each assigned a special branch of humanity to listen to and look after.

The low bass choir keeping gentle rhythm for the rising of the sun and the coming of seasons. Archangels belted and wailed ecstatically hoping to slow the genocides and put a morsel of bread in an empty stomach. The Angel's job was somewhere in between. She sung the prayers of desperate actresses, which intoned perfectly between hopeless poets and talentless street performers. She had sung so many prayers for so long that she fell in love with what she prayed for. She had no other choice. She had to incarnate. There were three buttons in the elevator and she pushed the middle one. It brought her to the intersection of Sunset and Vermont in Hollywood.

The audition room door slammed.

"No! Thank you!" yelled Jezebel Storm. The sound of her voice was tinged with the sugar of a forced smile. Jezebel Storm, stalked through the waiting room, a mask of good natured felicity slipping from where she had screwed it onto her face. She stopped in front of The Angel, sized her up in a glance, and aped with a schoolgirl whine:

"Good luck." Jezebel Storm sneered and stomped out of the room.

The Angel blinked. Her smile faded.

"Allie Osborne?"

The turtle shaped man called from down the hallway. The golden chimes of the prayer stopped abruptly in The Angel's heart. Allie Osborne pulled herself onto her oversized feet and gave the hem of her top one last tug. The Angel and Allie Osborne made eye contact one last time.

The Angel, mouthed "Good Luck."

Allie mouthed "Thank you."

A silence in a typhoon. The Angel hummed a prayer under her breath for Ms. Osborne. She knew that someone in the choir would do her a solid and take care of it for her.

Allie Osborne took a step towards The Angel and said:

"You look more like an angel than anyone in this room any way." All of the blonde heads snapped to attention. An offended gasp escaped the room. The water dispenser *glugged*. Deafening silence.

The Angel felt surprised and embarrassed. Did someone know? All of the blondes in the room crucified The Angel with their eyes as Allie Osborne turned on her large heel and walked into the audition room.

2

The room was dark. A key light cast a spot of brilliant white light onto the carpet, and the rest of the room was dipped in twilight shadow. Behind a plastic table the turtle shaped casting director peered through his gold-rimmed glasses at the headshot, under which was written the name 'Angel'. He sighed and turned the page over to look at her resume

It read:

Cherubim Choir - Alto
Seraphim Choir - Second Mezzo Soprano
Divine Principality - Middle American Continent
Human Qualifier - Los Angeles District West Hollywood North Hollywood, Burbank, Studio City

Below that was written several unintelligible symbols that appeared to be either the Greek alphabet or the font Wingdings.

The casting director cleared his throat and leaned his ample body back in his chair. It creaked under his weight. He had a brief daydream about working with his brother's logging company in Northern California. He wondered if he would feel different with hardened hands. He wondered if his brother thought about his own career as a casting director in the city of Hollywood. He ran his stubby fingers across the matte print headshot. He took note of her white gold hair, her perfectly pink upturned lips and her glacial blue eyes. He detested every molecule of her. The saccharine perfection of her made his sizable stomach lurch. He wished he could tear the picture to shreds, but he was after all, being paid. The producers didn't appreciate his personal feelings.

After a deep inhalation, he bellowed, "Angel!"

He tossed the headshot onto the table and slapped a button on a camera that was sitting on a tripod in the corner of the room. The Angel walked through the door as the camera whirred to life.

"Hi." The casting director bleated, adjusting the focus of the camera. He framed her brilliant face.

"Hello!" said The Angel with a smile that warmed the room several pleasant degrees.

"Ready?" he asked, zooming in tight on her face.

"Ready."

The Angel took a deep breath looked into the camera and stated, "I am Angel."

The casting director blinked a couple of incredulous times.

"Not in character right now."

"But, I am... I am Angel. It's my-"

"Do you have your side of the script?"

"I do, yes."

"Good, we can take it whenever you're ready. I'm going to be reading the part of the Vampire."

"And, I'll be the Angel."
"Yeah. That is the idea."
Then the camera rolled.

> Open on ANGEL, a beautiful woman with unfolded SILVER WINGS. She has a SWORD pressed to the throat of a VAMPIRE. A stream of blood runs from the vampire's mouth as he speaks

VAMPIRE
 I know who you are Angel! The Book of Shadows will never open for you!

ANGEL
 I have thrown off my feather wings and replaced them with my silver wings OF WAR! So that I can kill motherfuckers like you!

VAMPIRE
 The crystal will shatter upon your heavenly touch!

ANGEL
 I'm not in Heaven any more.

> The Angel JABS the vampire through the heart with her ENORMOUS SWORD. The Vampire's body, lights on FIRE, and explodes!

Give us this day our daily blood.

The Angel finished wiping pretend blood from her face and turned to the casting director. As she smiled at him, a bit of acid touched the casting directors heart. After seeing perfect blondes for hours on end he had begun to detest them. A sunset is only a sunset because it doesn't last all day.

"Can we try it again?" giggled The Angel, loving this.

The casting director reframed the shot, and stopped recording. The whirring in the camera died. The room was deadly silent. He felt sweat bead on his palms and wiped his hands through his thinning hair.

"No, it was fine."

"Can I try it one more time? Please."

"No. Your reading was fine. But the producers..."

He mentioned the name of the producers, as if invoking the name of a dark pagan god. Something faceless and mighty that had bestowed a small fiefdom upon him.

"The producers," he continued, "would like to see the role topless."

The casting director adjusted his glasses and wiped his palms on his jeans. He folded his hands over his belly and sat back in his folding chair. The producers had never said such a thing. In fact, he had never spoken directly to them. He had no desire to see her or anyone else topless. He just wanted tribute.

The Angel felt the eyes of the casting director on her, searching her human flesh. A violin string of terror plucked in her belly. This time, she did not thrill at her newfound emotions.

"I didn't know that it would be like this," she said, stifling a rising sensation to run.

"I didn't either, but that's what they want. And they're the producers. They sign the checks. We have to do what they want. You understand?"

"What if I don't?"

"The producers know what they want in an angel. If you're not an angel, you're not an angel, I guess. There are others." The casting director sat back in the creaking chair. Lights from the ceiling reflected off his glasses and blocked out his eyes entirely.

The Angel thought about the girl with the big feet. The Angel wished that she could pray. She knew well, that her space in the choir was empty. No one would be listening to her. She undid the top button of her blouse. She thought about the demon's bite on the hand of her Eternal Work Coach.

Thank the producers, thought the casting director, as the blouse fell to the floor.

3

The Angel walked out of the room feeling more naked than when her top was on the floor. Another blonde was sitting in the chair that she had been sitting in. Had it not been for the smell of hairspray, she could have imagined that she was in Heaven again. She walked through the room and no one noticed her. Earth was like heaven but silent in the wrong places. She muttered "Good luck," to the room and hurried to leave.

She stepped out onto the curb and was immediately assaulted by the sound of the traffic. She wanted, she wanted, she wanted... something. She wanted to be filled. She wanted to sleep or eat fast food, none of which she had tried. She wanted to smile, or dance, or explore the limits of her body. She still felt the eyes of the casting director on her. Her once infinite and perfect form felt like a common rag. She pushed the thought out of her mind and decided on fast food.

A pothole in the sidewalk caught her ankle and sent her tumbling down. The Angel fell to the concrete. The next thing she knew she lying on her back looking up at the deep California sky. She thought about lying there for a while and maybe trying to sleep.

"Hey," a small voice sounded from above her as a face came into her field of vision, blocking out the sun. The girl with the big feet hovered over her. The sun framed her face, and made even her hawkish nose look sweet. She offered a hand to The Angel and pulled her up.

Allie Osborne, the girl with the big feet, dug in the pockets of the ugly sweatshirt she was wearing and came up with a pack of cigarettes. She pulled one out with her mouth, lit it and spoke with it dangling from her lips.

"That pothole got me, too. Scraped my knee. I haven't scraped my knee in forever." She let a plume of smoke out of her nose.

"Me neither, I haven't scraped my knee in forever," said The Angel dusting herself off.

"Yeah, it's weird the things that you did all the time as a kid. Suddenly, you're not a kid any more." She trailed off and dragged on her cigarette "Did he try and get you to take off your shirt, too?" asked Allie, cutting her eyes towards The Angel.

"Yes."

"Yeah, me too."

"Did you do it?" asked The Angel.

"Yeah," said Allie, offering The Angel a cigarette.

"Me too," said The Angel, taking the cigarette.

"I was thinking of calling my agent or reporting him to the Actors Guild."

"I was thinking of getting fast food."

Allie looked at The Angel square in the face, she tossed her cigarette into the street and crushed it out.

"Yeah, fast food is a better idea. Let's just do that."

4

The Angel was lost in rapturous ecstasy. Her heartbeat quickened. Small droplets of sweat collected on her forehead. A tiny moan escaped from her mouth and for a moment the thin but impermeable membrane between heaven and earth seemed to part before her eyes.

Taco Bell held more glory than she had ever imagined. A small mountain of wrappers had grown on her tray. She paused consuming tacos and burritos only to politely order more, or refill her cup with a mixture of soda from each of the fountains.

Allie looked on with an equal combination of awe, respect and jealousy. She pulled on the straw of her child-sized iced-tea, making a squeaking noise. The Angel continued her assault on the pile of tacos uninterrupted.

"How, do you look like that?" The Angel halted her onslaught and chewed her mouthful of taco thoughtfully.

"I mean," continued Allie, "you seem to really like fast food. I'm sorry, I don't mean that how it sounded. That sounded really mean. People think I'm mean sometimes. I'm not. I'm just bluntish. You really like Taco Bell though."

"Doesn't everybody like these?" asked The Angel holding up half a taco.

"Well, yeah. But no one wants to get fat. I stopped eating bread for like a year this one time. I still don't keep it in my place."

"Why would you do that?" The Angel asked, putting her taco down gently. "Bread is great."

"Carbs."

"What are carbs?"

Allie stopped, stone silent.

"Are you new here?" she asked.

"Very new."

"Where are you from?" asked Allie.

The Angel looked down at her taco. She didn't know what to say. She didn't want to lie.

"Up north. Where are you from?" she asked lifting the taco back to her mouth.

"Here. I'm from here. But, nobody is actually FROM here, so people usually think that it's weird."

"I don't think that it's weird. That's nice."

Allie jabbed her straw into her iced tea, "Okay, what is it with you? Are you a Scientologist? Because, just tell me right now if you are a Scientologist."

"I don't know what that is."

"You're obviously not on some juice fast."

"No," The Angel began to worry that her new friend was agitated. Allie took a sharp breath through her nose.

"Are you trying to get me to come to your yoga studio? What do you want from me!? No one is nice for no reason. You are VERY nice! You are a very nice person."

"I thought that we were going to be friends," said The Angel polishing off her final taco.

Allie stopped like she had been slapped across the face. It was dumbfounding to see someone who legitimately did not have an ulterior motive. She had ceased to believe such a person existed in the world. Yet, here she was, annihilating a pile of tacos.

"Okay. Yeah, let's be friends. I'm okay with that." Allie said warily.

The Angel looked up and smiled, bright and beautiful.

"Nice to meet you Allie."

"I'm sorry, I forgot your name."

"I never told you. It's Angel. I was thinking of changing it to Doris or Phyllis."

"Wow... Just wow."

The Angel got up to refill her cup with soda from each fountain.

5

Twilight was burning the pale blue afternoon into a deep purple. A couple of stars winked in the upper atmosphere. A crush of cars clotted Santa Monica Boulevard. The Angel walked along the sidewalk drinking in the carbon monoxide. A homeless man with no legs argued with a transvestite. A prostitute in a short blonde bob crouched on the street corner awaiting a

John. A man with a burned face skateboarded by, trailing a fog of marijuana smoke.

She couldn't wait until this was her home. She couldn't wait until she was no longer a visitor. In this new world of tacos and potholes she wanted a small bit of real estate. In her first week as a human she had made a friend, she had been considered beautiful. She auditioned for a movie and she smoked a cigarette.

She wanted to throw herself into the city, to grab fistfuls of it and swallow them whole. She wanted its grime under her new fingernails and its brightness in her new veins.. She wanted its black and white, and all the grey in between. She declared genocide on her past.

The Angel came to the front door of her apartment. She had paid for a weeks rent to a man behind a bulletproof window. She pushed the buzzer, and someone grumbled on the other side. The heavy metal gate clicked open and she was greeted with the sickly green interior of the Harvey Arms on Santa Monica Boulevard.

In the morning the building vibrated with the sounds of daytime television and mothers cooing in Spanish to their babies. It smelled like cigarette smoke and cooked meats. People distracted by the practicalities of existence. As she mounted the stairs that night she heard the cacophony of prayers spiraling up through the stairwell like torn pages of a hymnal caught in a tornado.

They were the desperate ones, the prayers that most angels feared. While some prayers sounded like chimes or bells, these sounded like metal scraping on stone and grinding gears. They screamed. Only the battle-scarred angels of the old times had the strength to listen to the prayers, and look for one worth answering. It was like letting molten lead flow through your fingers until you found a pearl.

The desperate prayers fell upon Angel's ears. She slapped her hands to block out the sound but it just made them louder. She began to run. She threw herself up the stairs. The cigarette burned carpet whipped by her as she ran to her third floor studio apartment.

Tell me Sharon's not pregnant. She's got to be lying. If she is I don't know what I'll do.

The prayers flew like hatchets from the dark corridors.

Let me find some money tomorrow, or I'm gonna get sick again. I just need a little bit, and I don't wanna have to hurt nobody.

She planted her foot on the top step, her apartment within sight.

Don't let him find me. God please don't let him find me. If he does I'll just take the pills. I'll just take all of the pills. Please don't let me take them. I want to. I want to so badly, and I don't know if I can make it through the night.

A cold claw wrapped around her beating heart and squeezed. She fell to the ground sobbing next to her door, her keys balled up in her fist.

Please help me make it through the—

"Stop!" she shrieked, squeezing her eyes shut against the prayers.

The door across from The Angel's apartment creaked open. A man with a baldhead and tattoos creeping up his neck appeared illuminated by the dingy light of his apartment. He eyed her up and down and then and vanished into his apartment. When he returned, he placed a half finished roll of toilet paper next to the crying angel.

Please make this chick stop crying so I can go to sleep... I mean... Help her... If you can. Thanks. I mean... Amen.

6

Over the hill in North Hollywood Allie was walking when she promised herself that she would be running. In her head she ran three miles a day. In reality she ran for twenty minutes while listening to Beyoncé, and than walked the rest of her route, also listening to Beyoncé. Sometimes she would dance a little bit if no cars were passing her. She used to dance as a kid. She remembered the joy of pointing a toe and spotting a pirouette. Sometimes when she was alone she would stand in fifth position and attempt a pirouette. She was always disappointed that she couldn't spin like she used to.

She remembered her mother claiming that she was able to do four pirouettes on each leg. That was what Allie strove for. Her parents, long divorced, and both actors of varying success, would take turns picking her up from dance class where she fought for four pirouettes on each leg. Her parents made sure never to meet in the parking lot of the dance studio. They always asked about the car the other one was driving.

They fought by comparing resumes and scoring credits on IMDB. One day Allie showed her mother four wobbling pirouettes on each leg. Her mother said as a child she was able to do five as she looked at herself in the dance studio mirror. Allie stopped taking dance after that.

Tonight she wasn't dancing or running, she was gazing up at the endless North Hollywood avenue. Camarillo Street was lined with the faceless apartment blocks. On a street of a hundred thousand windows she felt invisible enough to run, to sweat, to dance, to be as ugly as she wanted.

Allie thought about Angel: Angel had said that it was nice that she came from this city. Angel said she was from up north, not San Francisco, maybe Petaluma, or Redding. She's too pretty for that. Angel looks like she had never eaten a carb in her entire life. Angel's name was Angel. I guess that is not so weird. I wonder how old Angel is. I guess she looked like she was in her twenties.

Genetics. She has amazing genetics. Some people have fantastic genetics, like those trainers who have infomercials on TV. I'll never look like them any way. I'm too fat and lazy. Honestly, if I could go just a week on one of those juice things. Or if I could get the stomach flu. I'd love to get the stomach flu, just like, super intense for a week. I just want to see what I would look.

I should be running. I bet Angel is running right now, or doing some crazy yoga. I can't believe that she doesn't have a phone. God. Like I would call her what would I say, "Oh hey, Angel, this is Allie. We got sexually harassed together. Do you want to go out for martinis?"

Angel is my friend. She told me that we were friends...

I don't remember the last time that I made a new friend...

Allie, without even realizing it had made it back to her apartment building. She clicked off her iPod and unstrapped it from her arm. Her cell phone was glowing on the bed where she had left it. She had a text message from her agent:

Call back: Tomorrow, Angel movie. Good Job Allie :)

"No. Way," Allie said to an empty apartment.

She tried a pirouette. She landed in a collapsed fifth position. She stood up straight and bowed to an invisible audience. She went to shower with her prayers answered.

7

> Open on Angel. The Angel is standing on a precipice over the BLOODKNOT GULL, the Vampire City. she is sharpening her sword with a holy whet stone. ALISTAIR the vampire prince of the high moon gazes down restringing his bow.

ALISTAIR
　If we go down there it will certainly mean death Angel. You know nothing of death.

ANGEL
　When you hear the prayers of someone on their dying bed for eternity you begin to understand. Perhaps not the way a vampire understands.

> Alistair is hurt by this. He gazes off into the full moon. His beautiful alabaster skin shimmers in the moon.

> The Angel approaches him.

I know that you did not choose what you are. No more than I chose what I am. If we do not find the crystal it will mean the death of both of our worlds. This may be the last moonrise that you and I see. Put down your bow vampire. Let me see how cold your touch is.

ALISTAIR
　I have always loved you!

> They begin to make love, the same way that they have fought. With fury, and passion, wailing with ecstasy.

"Alright! Nice! That was nice!" The director rambled from behind the casting table.

"I liked the way you, you know, really got into it. You go there. I appreciate people who go there!"

Allie was straddling the actor who was reading the part of Alistair. In her passion she mounted him in the middle of the casting office. She was making out with him filled with fury and passion, as the script dictated. She wiped some of the eyeliner he was wearing off of her cheek.

The director, who looked like he was sixteen years old, slapped on some sunglasses and hopped up onto the table. He swung his feet around. He addressed Allie and the guy that Allie was straddling.

"Now listen: okay? These books are hot. I mean you've read them. We've got EVERYONE with these books. We're going to keep the rating under PG-13 if we can. BUT we're going to tell the story you know? Tweens, teens, inbetweeners, twentysomethings, flirty-thirties, DIRTY-thirties, and of course the forgotten forties. These books have something for everyone okay? And everyone is connected so that means that we've got butts in seats. That means that the movie is going to be BIG! I'm talking BIG now! That's why we're going with unknowns. You're unknown. No one knows you. No one at all."

Allie, and the actor nodded in agreement. The director paused. He took his sunglasses off. He put them on again. He took them off again, and seemed as if he were about to say something. He clapped his hands.

"We'll let you know! Nice work guys! You can probably get off of him now."

Allie rolled off of the actor and helped him up. They smiled awkwardly at one another.

"You still have some eyeliner on you," said the actor gesturing to her face.

"Thanks it was good to work with you." Allie said quickly and opened the door to leave. As she walked towards the waiting room Allie buzzed with excitement. She wondered if this would be the moment that her life changed forever. She imagined herself talking to an enraptured audience about not giving up on your dreams, and being who you really are. She thought:

It went well, it went really well. God, I don't remember the last time that someone touched me. It wasn't legitimate, and he had a script in his hand, but you know- it was something. I have to get out more. *God, please let me book this. God please let me book this. God if you-*

"ALLIE! Hi! Do you remember me?"

It was Angel. Allie's heart and stomach collided. Angel jumped up and threw her arms around Allie. The hug felt perfect. Angel's skin smelled like lilac and talcum powder.

Angel pulled back from the embrace and dramatically put her hands on her hips eyeing Allie. "It's Angel!"

"Yeah! I mean, of course I remember you Angel. How are you? I didn't think that I'd see you again, do you have a phone yet?" Allie looked at Angel, something was different. She was still perfectly gorgeous, but it seemed that someone had dimmed the light behind her eyes just a bit.

"Are you okay?" Allie asked, concerned.

"Yes. Of course- I'm just kind of tired. Getting used to sleeping. Here."

"ANGEL? Is there an Angel here?" The voice of the casting director droned skeptically.

Allie cocked her head back to the Angel.

"Is that for you?" she asked. The Angel smiled, blinding Allie with a perfect row of white teeth.

"Yes," said Angel rolling her eyes.

"ANGEL? No last name given!?"

The Angel looked towards the door and Allie, stepped aside.

"Go, go, you go, but... um... Do you want.." Allie trailed off. She knew what she wanted to ask but had no idea how to ask it. Angel leaned forward expectantly.

"I want you to come and have a drink with me tonight. I want to celebrate. Celebrate our callbacks," blurted Allie.

"Of course!"

"Formosa Cafe. Nine."

"I'll find it... Wish me luck!" And with that The Angel turned and walked into the room. Allie heard a muffled, "Is that your real name?" followed by, "I'm thinking of changing it to Phyllis."

God... please don't let her get this role.
God... please let her be my real friend.

8

Formosa Café was a hold over from The Golden Age of Hollywood. It was all leather booths and wood paneling below headshots of dead actors. Clarke Gable, Greta Garbo, and Bozo the Clown smiled at the swarming mass of twenty-somethings below. The bar was packed with hair gel and print t-shirts, with thick framed glasses and ironic facial hair. Women tried to look younger and men tried to look richer. Everybody tried to look like somebody. There was the smell of hairspray, gin, and a waft of cigarette smoke. Looking down on all of it, in the fluorescent perfection were the black and white headshots of stars that had ceased to shine.

Allie sat at the bar nervously chewing ice and knocking back gin and tonics. She wore a white blouse, black pants, glasses, and a shrug. It was too hot for the shrug but she wanted to round off all of her rough edges. She wanted to sit with Angel at the bar and be entirely beyond approach. She wanted to be beautiful by association. Then someone pushed her aside to order a drink filling her nostrils with cheap cologne and body odor.

Allie was two drinks deep when the Angel squeezed through the door looking radiant in a simple white dress. She looked tired. For a moment, Angel looked average. Forgettable even. Allie waved Angel over.

It was late. She was glad to have an excuse not to be in her apartment. She was glad not to hear the desperate prayers powerlessly until she forced herself to sleep. She was in a bar. It was late. It was loud. She could lose herself here. Angel's toes curled in delight. Everything was new.

"Hey!" Allie yelled over the noise of the bar.

"Hello!" Angel hugged her and took the stool next to Allie. The bartender attended to her immediately. She ordered a glass of wine.

Allie, began rambling and swirling a gin and tonic. She cast her eyes down the bar, looking for someone who was maybe looking for her. She didn't want to meet anybody; but she didn't want to not meet anybody. She wanted to be seen with Angel.

"I mean. I don't know WHO is making these decisions. I assume that it's a shadowy figure who sits behind a huge desk. Who knows? I don't know. But you're new to town and you got a call back! I think that is CRAZY!" Allie sucked an ice cube into her mouth and crunched it into snow.

"Thanks, Allie. Congratulations to you too!"

"And so like- when I saw you... Like, when I SAW you, and you wanted to go out and get fast food and stuff. I don't know. I just kind of thought that you were in a cult or something."

"Why!?" Angel yelled over the dull din of top 40 hits and bar chatter.

"Because you're nice," Allie said, scootching closer so Angel didn't have to yell. The smell of talcum and lilac breezed across her once again, and something moved in Allie, a bit of a drop, a small swell, and a hard swallow.

She took a breath and chose her words.

"Not many people are nice here. Not for no reason." Allie's lips almost grazed Angel's ear. For a brief second she thought about slipping one of Angel's white earlobes between her teeth. Allie, recoiled at her own thought and looked down the bar again for an unshaved chin and broad shoulders.

"I'm nice for no reason." A baritone voice appeared in back of the women. They both turned to notice an impish man in a fedora with a goatee and a hip cocked casually to the side. Allie would have been able to hold in a laugh if she had not already downed three gin and tonics.

"Great!" Angel exclaimed extending her hand to the little man.

"This is Allie, I'm Angel. We're friends."

"I'm Burt, everybody calls me Burt."

"Hey, Burt," said Allie crunching into some ice.

"What are you ladies drinking?"

"Alcohol," said Allie, and Burt's gaze turned on a dime to Angel. Burt squinted his eyes and put two fingers to his temple.

"So you're... Woah," he put a finger to his temple."

"I'm a little psychic, and I'm getting a strong impression from you." Allie rolled her eyes so hard that it hurt.

"You're an actress?"

"Yes! Wow! I mean, I hope to be some day," Angel said full of reverent humility.

Burt took the stool next to Angel without invitation and ordered her another wine in spite of her full glass. Angel leaned in and listened to Burt as he went on about a "big project" that he was working on. Allie was jealous and drunk.

She caught her own eyes in the mirror across from the bar. She got a call back today. She got a call back today for a big movie. If she got a part in a big movie everything would change. She thought about what her life would be like, when everything changed. She lifted a finger to the bartender.

"Another gin and tonic."

"I've never had a shot before," she could hear Angel say to Burt. Allie sucked another gin soaked ice cube into her mouth. She bit down hard.

9

Angel was doused in crimson light. Her white dress and skin dyed twilight sanguine in the fading bulb. A slight smile slurred across her lips and she ran a single pearlescent finger down her long neck. She saw herself in the full-length vanity in the ladies restroom. She realized that she hadn't heard a single prayer. Her smile deepened. She realized that the voices had stopped. She realized that she was drunk. She realized that she had never seen her reflection in heaven. She had never felt so far from it. She wondered if it had ever happened. She took a step towards the mirror.

The door muffled the sounds of the bar, and the dim red light made her feel like she was floating in nothingness. She thought of the night prayers in her apartment building. She wondered if she drank enough that she would never hear them again. She wanted the oblivion of this moment to last forever. She wanted to lose herself in something. She wanted to lose herself in anything.

She wanted to vomit.

The door pushed open, and Allie staggered in.

"It says 'dolls' on the door, like Guys and Dolls. That's a cute bathroom door. I'm going. I mean: I'm going to pee and then I'm going to leave, it's late. Are you and uh, the little guy..."

"Burt?"

"Yeah, Burt." She chuckled as she slammed the door of the stall shut and sat down.

"I don't know where he is." The tinkle of urine hitting water began in the stall.

"Probably just as well, he seemed super rape-y,"

Allie washed her hands and dried them on the legs of her pants. She took notice of Angel staring at herself in the mirror. She stood behind her. They talked through the mirror, placing strands of hair behind ears and smoothing out blouses.

"If I were you, I would always be in front of a mirror. Is that petty? It's shallow, I know. I can see why you don't have any other girlfriends."

That stung angel a bit.

"I'm new here," she said.

"You're a really sweet person. And, I'm your friend?" Allie asked. Angel nodded. Allie noticed something in her eyes, a bit of fear, a shard of sadness that wasn't there before.

"What's wrong?"

"I don't want to go home alone." Angel stared at Allie through the mirror. Allie swallowed hard. She felt immediately too sober and too drunk. She looked at the back of Angel's thick blonde hair, she wanted to bury her fingers in it. Everything was new.

"I... Just don't like being alone there," Angel continued, a slight quivering beginning in her chin.

Allie took a step towards Angel. She was close enough to smell the talcum and lilac, and wine and cigarettes. A new hunger roused in her.

"Will you come home-" Angel turned towards Allie and hands were buried in her hair. Lips were softly crushed on lips. Allie's mouth was cold and tasted like gin. A spark had caught and they burned to cinders as neither woman pulled away. Allie caught sight of them in the mirror, and for a moment, bathed in the monochromatic red light, she couldn't tell who was who.

10

When Angel's eyes popped open. Allie was next to her, naked except for a single sock on her left foot. The night before came back to her in flashes. A swerving car ride. Allie dead silent behind the wheel. A hand on a thigh. High heels removed. Stairs run up barefoot. A key drunkenly searching for its lock. A bed. Clothes. Skin. Sin. It was a deathblow. A black mark on her heart. A small deadly cancer. Could she go back again? Go back where? Hadn't she always been here?

A headache and an avalanche of nausea doused her like a cold bucket of water thrown over her naked body. She jumped up to vomit in the bathroom.

Her body heaved its contents into the toilet and she felt better for a moment. She sat naked on the floor of her bathroom, unaware of how to proceed. There was a naked woman in her bed and she had been incarnate for less than a month. She thought about her Eternal Work Coach with the demon bite on his hand. She ran unconscious hands across her body looking for where she had been bitten. The murky memories played before her eyes, each half bitter, half delicious. The muscles in her hips ached lusciously. Her lips were swollen and every movement woke a sweet kind of ache in her body. She didn't know what it was but she wanted more. She moved to her feet, approaching the bathroom door.

She pushed the door open, wishing the hinges more silent than they were. She looked at Allie from the safe distance of her bathroom. A pile of dirty blonde hair, and waves of hips and shoulders buried deep in tussled sheets. Her makeup had rubbed off leaving a freckled, flushed face. It was the face of someone who played outdoors. The face of a good kid. This was not the face of a demon, this was not the face of sin. Angel was incredibly confused.

Before she knew it Angel was lifting the sheets and examining every inch of Allie, the slow curve of her spine, her gently rounded butt, the roll of inviting flesh around her mid section. Angel wanted her body next to Allie's. She wanted to be encircled by her entirely. She had no idea why.

Allie rolled over on her side. Angel lifted the sheets and got in bed. She put her head on the pillow. Allie's hair was spilled across it like a can of dirty blonde paint. Angel crept an arm across Allie's waist, and unconsciously Allie took a hold of it, weaving their fingers together and clutching them to her chest.

Angel heard a small golden chime sound drowsily in the distance.

Thank you. Please let this be real. Don't let her leave me. She prayed, and Angel clutched Allie tighter. Angel hummed her prayer up through the crumbling roof to the Heavens. If this was sin, it was what she wanted.

Allie's eyes cracked open, and she smelled talcum and lilac. She felt soft arms around her. She drew them around her like a protective cape.

"Are you really my friend, Angel?" Her voice was fried to a crisp.

"Yes."

"Thank you."

11

They went shopping for a phone. Allie put the glowing screen into Angel's hand and began pointing out how to use it. Angel's eyes boggled at the magic in the palm of her hand. Allie took the device and put her number in it. Angel had one contact according to the phone. This was enough for Angel.

They walked down Hollywood Boulevard. Angel poked the dingy brass stars with her toe. They hiked up Runyon Canyon until Allie was soaked through with sweat. They ate overpriced salads while wearing large sunglasses. With every new experience there was a smile that glittered across Angel's face. She discovered everything anew from the topography of the bizarre on Melrose, to the sleek lines and overstated cool of Sunset Boulevard.

The streets began to become characters of their own, new friends for Angel to meet. She saw her new friends' names in the signs that came whizzing by on the 101 Freeway. Allie began to see her city through Angel's eyes. For a moment every dirty curb and hard angle was blessed with novelty.

When they returned, sunburnt and delirious from craning their necks to look at the soaring buildings downtown, they fell into bed at Angel's apartment and slowly entwined themselves, learning and relearning every curve and dip and fullness of each other's bodies. They fell into one another from undeniable gravity. Allie loved Angel's hands exploring every inch of her body. She felt remade, new again, beautiful in the eyes of someone beautiful.

One night in between the whooshing of passing cars illuminating Angel's studio apartment on Santa Monica Boulevard, Allie thanked God saying in a prayer, *I love her. Thank you.*

Angel whispered, "I love you too," and Allie wondered for a moment if she had spoken her prayer aloud. She turned to meet Angel's gaze. Their eyes met in the darkness. They saw each other only when a passing car's headlights traveled across the room. They said nothing. They held each other in the darkness, waiting to see each other again in the traveling lights of a busy boulevard. They drifted off to sleep.

The morning poured in and Angel rested her face on the pillow next to Allie letting the smell of her hair envelop her. Their breath synced and neither said a word. They held each other in the six A.M. silence. As they slowly began to slip once again into the heaven of unconsciousness Allie's phone vibrated.

Allie let out a frustrated groan and dug through her pants, which lay crumpled on the floor next to the bed. Her eyes were still closed, trying to keep one foot in the dream world.

The glowing text on the screen read:

Final Callback Angel\Vampire Movie. Just you and one other girl. She's good but the casting director seems to think she might be crazy. It's next week. Maybe think about doing a juice fast or a cleanse. Have got a good recipe.

12

> Open on Angel, her back is turned to Alistair. A PLATINUM SWORD sticks out of his stomach. A thin rivulet of black blood streams from the side of his mouth. The Angel approaches, and puts a hand on the gleaming handle of the sword.

ALISTAIR
You will not finish me. You are too merciful. I've seen you fight, I've seen you win, but I've never seen you be cruel.

ANGEL
Perhaps this will be the first time. Perhaps I will surprise you. Now that the crystal is destroyed I have no more use for you demon.

ALISTAIR
It's demon now?

ANGEL
It was always demon. I do not apologize for breaking your heart, as it has not been beating for a long time.

ALISTAIR
And did you never love me? Did you never love me as you said you did?

ANGEL
I have only one lover.

ALISTAIR
  Your God?

ANGEL
  My sword. My mission. My God. They're all the same.

ALISTAIR
  Could you imagine a world where we could have been? Perhaps if we had been mere mortals. Could you imagine a world without your mission, without your God without-

            Angel leaps onto Alistair and digs the sword into his torso. BLOOD ERUPTS from his chest cavity COVERING The Angel completely. Close up on Angel. She is framed in the enormous disk of the vampire moon, blood dripping from her face. A single tear escapes her eye.

ANGEL
  No. I cannot imagine it. I cannot imagine a world without... my sword.

            Fade to black

            Credits.

            The End.

The casting room was cavernous. It sat on the top floor of a building on the corner of 7th and Francisco Street. Huge windows turned those watching the reading into shadows. The camera whirred, the director twitched, the casting director rested his hands on his belly. The producers sat, crossed legs and arms, faces blocked out by the late afternoon setting sun. At the center, a woman in a blood red jacket examined two pictures of two blonde women.

Angel finished her reading. Tears were streaming down her face. The young man playing Alistair was dead on the floor, impaled with a cardboard tube. The room had fallen silent. The director did a double take back to the producers who gave him the slightest of nods.

"Nice. Nice. Nice. Nice. Very nice work. Is it Angel or Phyllis now?"

Angel wiped tears from her face.

"Whatever it says on my headshot."

The director laughed. "Don't you love her? I told you, you would love her. I love her. You're great. I think this is all we need. Is Jeremy still dead over there?"

Everyone in the room looked to the actor lying corpse still on the ground, the cardboard tube sticking straight up.

"Jeremy, Hey! Jeremy, look how method he is! Jeremy you can come back to life now." Jeremy sat up, the cardboard tube still in his armpit. The director looked back to the producers. The woman in the red jacket nodded.

"That's all we need from you Angel, it's been great getting to know you! Can you send in ummm..." The director snapped his fingers, searching his memory.

"Allie?"

"Yeah, give us a couple of minutes and then send her in okay? This is exciting! Isn't this exciting?" The director glanced between the producers and Angel, a puppy ready to eat.

Angel looked towards the casting director. His eyes were invisible behind the glare of his glasses.

"Thank you," he mumbled, under his breath.

"Thank you for the opportunity," said Angel. She turned to leave. Her heels click clacked on the marble floor as she walked out of the room. Each step was a marathon. She wanted to sleep, she wanted to crawl into warm sheets beside Allie, she wanted to crumple in to herself and turn into dust. For every night that she had not spent with Allie, she found solace from the night prayers in a bottle of something strong. She opened the door to the waiting room. Allie sat, straight as an arrow, eyes focused hard on the door, as if she were trying to see through it.

Allie had fasted and exercised militaristically for the last week. When she ran she ran hard, when she ate she ate little. She focused on this, just this moment, just the people behind that door. She was wedged into new clothes and caked with makeup. She looked like a well-dressed weapon.

Angel wanted to rush into her arms, but she didn't. Allie refused her for the week before the audition. Angel checked and rechecked her new cellphone. She found no messages from her only contact.

"They want you in a couple of minutes."

"Okay." Allie said, and then twisted her lips into a tight knot. Angel folded her script and put it in her purse. She sat several seats away from Allie and pretended to go through her new phone. She scrolled the screen up and down. She turned it off and on. She looked at Allie's number.

"You should go home. You look tired," said Allie after a moment of cutting silence.
"I was going to wait for you."
"Really. I'll be fine. I'll call you later."
"Maybe we can go out for tacos?"
"I'll call you later."

A voice came from down the hall. "Allie?"
Allie snapped up straight. She squared her headshot and resume. She pulled her blouse down and hitched her breasts. She walked to the door. She walked towards the room. She walked towards the eyes of those with the idea, those with the script, those with the money. She walked towards her future. Each step felt like leaving one life for another. If Allie Osborne could hear prayers, if she could hear the silvery trumpet belt of prayers, she would hear Angel praying as loudly as possible, to whoever could hear.

Please, let her get this part. Please let her come back to me.

13

Allie booked the role of the angel. Allie played the Angel. Angel changed her name to Phyllis and got a job waitressing on Melrose. Allie would come into her restaurant sometimes. Each time something was a little different. Her nose was a little smaller. Her hair was a little blonder. Her waist narrowed. Ever so slowly she became unrecognizable from the freckle-faced girl in the bed. Angel's nametag said Phyllis, and Allie called her so. Every time Angel brought Allie her egg white omelet half of her hoped that Allie would recognize her, and the other half feared that she would.

Brunch was busy but everyone said that industry people came for brunch so she was lucky to be working that shift. She might get noticed. Nights alone became easier. She learned to ignore the cries of others and slowly stopped hearing them. She indulged in the occasional taco, but the caloric content was slightly more than she could justify. She did several student films, and had a walk on role in a pilot, but for the most part she kept her head down and stole glances at herself in the reflections of passing cars.

When the movie came out, Allie's face was 20 feet tall on billboards lining La Brea. Phyllis would look away from them as she passed by, instead turning her head to criticize her reflection in the windows of shops she could not afford.

One ink black Hollywood evening after more than a couple glasses of wine, Phyllis found herself in front of a movie theatre. She found herself in a chair. As the light dimmed around the late show audience she looked around. There was a couple feeding each other chocolates, teenagers passing a pipe between them, and a child leaning into the screen. She tried to hear a single prayer. She could hear nothing. She felt safe from harm in a midnight movie full of prayerless people.

An usher with a mechanical voice box said, "Enjoy the show." The lights went out. The movie flicked to life. Allie unfurled her wings. Phyllis began to weep.

L.A. History 2

The Abridged Corrected History of Los Angeles
"Revolutions"
1821-1849

By the early 1800s the small Spanish Pueblo established on the banks of the river of Los Angeles was gaining international attention for its temperate clime, beneficial trading position, and ability to bend natural law. Geologists believe that the slowly decaying bodies of angels in the Hollywood hills mixing with the demon-tainted water of the Los Angeles River creates a unique human experience for some while it drives others completely mad. This accounted for the noticeable rise in psychotic behavior and barbarism during a small rainstorm in Los Angeles. Municipal historian Jennie Anderton wrote in her 1984 Treatises on Mental Instability in Spanish Era Los Angeles:

"Of the original eleven founders still living in the newly established Pueblo of Los Angeles only eight survived. The three others were believed to be sorcerers who sought to rally the Indians against the Spanish cause in early Los Angeles. The three were drown in the river and left for dead. The bodies washed out to the Pacific Ocean and promptly returned to seek their revenge. Eventually, after being shot through with a cannon, hung, and then set ablaze they did not return from the grave. The remaining founders regarded one another with wary suspicion."

Peace descended upon the Los Angeles River Basin as the indigenous peoples began to form alliances with the Spanish settlers. The natives intermarried with Spanish settlers, seduced by their technology that verged on magic. The Spanish settlers accepted the marriages with the native population seduced by their magic that verged on technology. After the War of Angels and Demons the inhabitants of the Los Angeles Pueblo were forged anew by the fire of battle and weary of constant combat. Even The Great and Terrible Sea Monster living off of the coastline began allowing ships to approach without being sucked down to the depths to keep it company for all of eternity.

Intrusion

Boats docking in Santa Monica and San Pedro brought modern curios from Europe ranging from farming equipment to advanced calendars. The ships themselves were sailed by Moors, Serbs, Bulgars, Italians, French, Greeks and Turks. Along with the finery of Europe and the Middle East, they brought with them their own cultural knick-knacks. They unloaded jinns, trolls, witches, saints, the evil eye, and the occasional vampire all of whom found a place in the glittering sand and poisoned water of early Los Angeles. A separate peace was formed between the settlers along the river basin under the maxim that still exists today: everyone is dangerous, they should not be trusted, but they should be respected, befriend only the powerful so that you may become like them. And crush them.

Throughout the entirety of California, a Mexican identity was born. In 1821 Mexican Independence was declared and the Spanish flag was lowered. Remaining Spanish troops were cast into the ocean to feed The Great and Terrible Sea Monster and ensure their success as a nation through forming alliances with *the old ones*. Los Angeles was quickly becoming the beautiful and cursed jewel in the crown of the expanding Mexican empire. Then gold was discovered.

"The Mayan word for gold translates roughly to the excrement of the Gods. In fact, it would be more accurate to say that gold is the violent aphrodisiac of the Gods. The discovery of gold in Southern California roused the attention of the Confederation of United Freemasons. George Washington was the sitting Grand Dragon of the Confederated Freemasons. The United States of America had already conquered a swath of the East Coast after snapping the chains from their colonial masters in England. It is conventional wisdom that one not keep a tiger as a pet. Tigers grow up. Tigers who love gold don't exist. But if they did, they would be the most dangerous organism in the world. The events of the 1840s in Southern California would leave Mexico wishing that it had never retrieved gold from its land."

The Ever War

In 1846 after only two decades of relative peace the Mexican-American War erupted in California. The battle-hardened, blood-drunk, gold-seeking American troops led by Freemason commanders poured in from Northern California to seize the site of other-worldly power along the gateway to Hell.

Robert F. Stockton a 14th Degree Grand Elect Mason and Commodore of the American Army docked off San Pedro to launch an offensive on the Pueblo of Los Angeles. Now friendly to the Mexican cause, The Great and Terrible Sea Monster rose out of the sea with tentacles whipping. It drew men into the depths, and launched legions of undead Spanish conquistadores from the bottom of the ocean to attack the American Naval vessel. Stockton, battle-ready from the war of 1812 and familiar with the horrors of the deep from his time spent off of the coast of West Africa, was able to subdue The Great and Terrible Sea Monster. It receded into the depths, ashamed and sulking at its defeat by a mere mortal. In present day Santa Monica it can only be found rousing occasionally to snatch an unwitting beach goer.

Stockton marched on the Pueblo of Los Angeles and met with American armies from the unprotected Northern territories of Mexico. This led to the greatest human battle of Angelino history: the Battle for Los Angeles was fought in 1846.

The advanced Freemason technologies clashed with the ancient Indian magicks in the loose confederation of towns surrounding the river basin. Calling upon their ancient native powers, the Mexican citizens transformed into grizzly bears and wolves tearing American troops limb from limb as they tried to reload their Springfield rifles. The U.S. Army countered the natives by unleashing cadres of vampires starved to the point of insanity. Because both sides had a reasonably Judeo-Christian bent, the angels and demons stood by. They watched and waited. God also observed patiently to see which side showed the least mercy to the other, and therefore, the most love for him. Still Stockton was pushed back to his boat in San Pedro Harbor.

In a letter to U.S. Secretary of State, and fellow Freemason Daniel Webster, Stockton wrote

"The Mexicans are fearsome and determined, they would be a powerful asset to the illuminated ones of our order if only their spirits can be broken like the stallions of Arabia. The gold will be ours for the glory of our order and the all-seeing eye. Provisions of hardtack, ammunition, gunpowder, and tallow must be provided posthaste in order to regroup and further molest the savages. If it is not being used elsewhere, The Amulet of Ra would help in our bloody effort. From many let there be one."
-Robert Stockton 1843 October

The Amulet of Ra was unable to be sent by the Continental Army as it was being used elsewhere. It is assumed to glow quietly in the desk of the current president, waiting for its awesome power to be unleashed.

The Final Blow

Stockton Marched on Los Angeles from the south while U.S. forces in the north inched ever closer to the glorious Pueblo on the River. They carried with them modern weaponry, superior military tacticians, and several of The Horns of Jericho, which they fully intended on using. Upon seeing that they were surrounded, Acting Governor of Mexican Alta California, Andres Pico, bowed at the feet of his conquerors. The European educated Pico recognized the American commanders dressed in their traditional Freemason aprons and top hats. He was in no way interested in fighting high-order Freemasons. Primary sources claim that:

"Their hands were sheathed in pristine white gloves, clutching ceremonial swords, and their eyes rolled in ecstasy as they communed with their dark gods, offering sacrifice in exchange for victory."

Andres Pico's brother, Pio Pico, was a Los Angeles native and therefore a deformed giant. Having previously served as the Governor of California and in light of the fact that he was an actual deformed giant, Andres Pico thought his brother far better to bargain with the terrifying American Freemasons.

The mantle of power was shrugged off by Andres Pico and taken up by Pio. He served as the Governor of Mexican California for less than a year until he was forced to sign the Treaty of Cahuenga in 1847. A special pen was created for Pio Pico to sign the Treaty of Cahuenga. It was carved from the mast of one of the American sailing ships because, quote, "we're [they're] not going anywhere."

Pico served as Governor of California for less than a year, just long enough to make Los Angeles the municipal hub of California. He left Los Angeles after the signing of the Treaty of Guadalupe Hidalgo, which ended the Mexican-American War. After living away from Los Angeles for many years, he returned to a normal human size. He was quoted as saying, "It is always better to be a freakish giant in Los Angeles than a normal sized person anywhere else in the world."

Punksnotdead

24 Hours Remaining

At midnight Punk walked out of the ocean. He spat salt water from his blue lips. His *Black Flag* sweatshirt and jeans were drenched. He stepped onto the sand of Redondo Beach. He looked like a pile of wet laundry made animate. He spat more salt water on to the beach. He bent down and buried his hands in the sand. He pushed his hands deeper and deeper until his elbows was sunk in it. Water rushed around his crouching form as he removed his arm from the thick wet muck. He opened his pale hand in the moonlight. A small crab lay on it's back digging at nothing.

Punk smiled. He looked around.

The beach stretched out all around him. Cold, wet, California December. A breeze sucking off the ocean ran across his sea soaked face like razor blades. The pain, the sand, the crab, the night, the moon, they all felt good to him. He shivered a little in his oversized *Black Flag* sweatshirt. He was getting too cold. He needed to find his cross.

Punk hiked up the beach, his lungs sucking and gurgling. His legs felt like the churn of the ocean. His *Airwalk* shoes were leaden with freezing salt water. The orange sand of the beach was painted a pale blue by the silver dollar moon. He looked back at the waves crashing on the shore. He reached the bicycle path and walked along, trailing soggy footprints as he went.

He found his cross was stuck under an abandoned lifeguard tower surrounded by beach sweepers and bulldozers left to rust in the ocean air. He ducked into the darkness under the lifeguard tower and saw it. The cross was made of a skateboard deck, broken in half and nailed together. "Punk" was written in black Sharpie marker. He felt the ragged edges of his cross. He remembered the snap. He remembered the fall. The bite of the waves across his face. He touched his face and smiled, thrilling at the memory. Between sensation and nothingness, the choice was easy. He dropped to his knees.

He began to dig. His wet clothes were caked in sand by the time he found what he was looking for. They bought the footlocker at a military surplus store in San Pedro. He wondered if it was still there. If he had time he would go, but he didn't have time so he wouldn't. There was never enough time. He pulled the trunk onto the sand and positioned himself so he could see in the moonlight.

The footlocker screeched as he forced the battered hinges open. Neatly folded in the footlocker he found an oversized Black Flag sweatshirt identical to the one he was wearing. He found identical jeans, a Strung Out t-shirt, an identical pair of *Airwalks*, and a pair of black socks.

His clothes fell to the sand with a wet slop. The freezing water from the beach shower sunk its teeth into Punk's naked body. That felt good too. He opened his mouth and he tasted the gorgeous fresh water. It was almost sugar sweet compared to the acrid seawater. The grit coursed off of his body between his toes. His skin felt loose and scaly under his hands, or maybe it had always felt like that.

He wriggled, wet and cold, into his new clothes. Before he put his sweatshirt on he held it out and buried his face in it. A child rubbing his cheek with velvet until he fell asleep. An embrace on the first day of freedom from prison. It smelled perfect. The inside of a tennis ball can, an industrial detergent. Brand. New.

It fell over large down his slight frame and wrapped him like a mother's hug. A smile jumped onto Punk's face and he cast an eye toward the sea. He took a sip from the drinking fountain and spat into the ground. He returned to the footlocker and he pulled out his holy trinity:

1) The Discman: with oversized earphones attached.
Three CDs: Danzig- Live from the Black Hand Side
Black Flag- Nervous Breakdown
Strung Out- Twisted by Design

2) The weed: An eighth of thick purple\green nuggets of marijuana. He buried his face in the bag and soaked his face in the pungent odor.

3) The board: A nicely broken-in skateboard. Trucks as loose as he liked, and asphalt worn wheels. Worn down grip tape and deep grooves from grinding the concrete. A pretty board was an ugly board, and a worn board was a work of art.

He left his wet clothes in a black heap on the beach. He left the sea, shaking sand out of his new pant legs. He stepped onto the empty bicycle path to rolling drums, driving guitar, and Danzig crooning She Rides. He pulled his black hood over his head and turned up his music like a crow opening its wings. He pushed off his skateboard, and he flew.

The empty lifeguard towers and sleepy streets watched him as he pushed his board harder. He wanted to go faster than he ever had before. He was the salt wind and the ragged guitars. He was the note that Glen Danzig was screaming out at a million fans. Punk would never die.

He saw a dark figure on a skateboard approaching in the streetlights. Punk pushed harder, he turned his music louder. The figure brought his board to a stop under a flickering streetlight.

When he got to the pool of light, Punk burned-out his board, laying back and kicking up a wave of loose sand to stop. He kicked the board reflexively into his hand and slung it over his shoulder.

"You're late, dude," Punk said, his voice a salty rasp.

"Made me work longer if I wanted today and tomorrow off."

"Dude. Brad. You look the same," said Punk, pulling a crooked smile.

"Nah, man I'm getting old." They both knew it was true. For a moment they stood in the light examining one another. Brad tilted his straight brimmed ball cap up. He was handsome save for the patch of burn-scarred flesh tracing down the side of his face. Brad's skin was deeply tan even in the night. He had the solid build of someone used to velocity, with a frame to take the abuse. Punk was pale and slight. From under his hoodie thin platinum blonde hair fell over his forehead hiding his eyes. He was avian and delicate, with a face like china. He looked all of seventeen. He would never be any older or younger.

Without a word they moved into one another and hugged. Brad swallowed a knot that rose in his throat and he pounded Punk on the back with his large hands. Punk felt like a sack of bones wrapped in a sweatshirt. They pulled away from each other and Brad lowered his ball cap again, cutting a shadow over his eyes.

"How old are you now?" Punk asked, the low wet trill of the ocean in the background of his voice.

"Guess, man."

"What year is it?"

"Guess, man." Brad smiled broadly under the shadow of his cap. It wasn't worth his best friend coming back to life if he couldn't mess with him. Punk wound up dramatically and went to kick Brad playfully in the balls.

"Dude, I don't know! Just tell me!" Punk laughed as he connected with Brad's crotch.

"Oh shit! You totally connected," squeaked Brad, doubled over and dropped to his knees. "It's 2014, man. I'm 26. Shiiiiit... hold on, just give me a minute."

"15 years huh?"

"Welcome back," Brad wheezed.

"24 hours. Let's skate."

He stood up trying to cap the pain in his groin. He produced a joint, lit it in his mouth and handed it to Punk. Punk dragged deeply on it. He reveled in the dry fragrant smoke in his lungs. They felt the mild euphoria begin to seep over them. It was time.

The wheels scraped as they jumped onto their boards. Punk tucked his headphones under his hoodie. Brad popped in his ear buds and put on Sublime.

They rode in parallel lines down the bike path. They ground along benches, and ollied over pieces of driftwood. They carved lines in the stray sand blown over the bicycle path. They passed the joint effortlessly without missing a kickflip or a manual. They picked up a bottle of cheap whiskey like old times. The dead boy poured whiskey down his throat without a flinch.

If it weren't for Punk's cold, water wrinkled fingers. If it weren't for the sun lines that had creased Brad's eyes and the corners of his mouth; If it weren't for the taste of salt left on the rim of the bottle of whiskey; they would have thought that no time had passed at all. In a way it hadn't.

Brad thought about his girlfriend, and his car, which needed an oil change and to have its brake pads replaced. He thought about his job tending bar. He thought of all of the forgotten foundations of dreams that he and Punk had shared. He wondered if the dead boy was disappointed in him. He took another long drag on the joint and another belt from the bottle. He pushed his board until the night stretched over him like a blanket.

The dead boy thought of lying at the bottom of the ocean. He thought of the nothingness of the sea. He thought about the cold and the wet. He did not want to go back home. This was going to be the best 24 hours of his death.

3

Punk's name is not Punk. Punk's parents called him Peter. At least that's what his gravestone said on it. Brad gave him his real name on a sticky camp day in the summer between second and third grade.

The first day of summer camp at Rocket Ship Park, Punk stood staring up at the titular rocket after his mother dropped him off in a crush of minivans and SUVs. He wanted to go up in the ship. He could play some good pretend up there. A counselor grabbed him by his shoulders and shoved him into a group of 8- year-olds shiny with sunscreen and reeking of chemical coconut smell. The counselors wore t-shirts and claimed with sugar filled certainty that this was going to be the best summer ever. Punk was dragged pell-mell to a long table full of rainbow colored markers that smelled like fruit and chocolate if you inhaled deeply enough. A pear shaped girl with braces, enormous breasts, and fantastic pit stains jumped up and down behind the table saying:

"Let's all make nametags! And decorate them!"

Seeing no other alternative, 8-year-old Punk began decorating his nametag. They were told that juice would be given to them if they made their nametags extra pretty. The pear shaped girl smiled encouragingly as all of the children drew. She was very obviously a lover of juice.

Punk rushed through his design, his marker clutched in his fist. He was unable to get the colors that he wanted and had to settle for black and brown. He wanted the juice he was promised. When it became obvious that no one was going to share the good colors with him, he scribbled his name across the nametag. His name was barely legible and he worried that he would be refused juice for not making his name tag "extra pretty." He decided to draw a skateboard next to his name. Because skateboards were cool, and he wanted to be cool. He hoped that anyone seeing his nametag would assume that he was a cool guy who skateboarded (he didn't) and want to drink juice with him.

"Is your name Punk?" asked a boy from across the table attempting to read his poorly scribbled name. The boy had accidental red and green lines drawn under his nostrils from excessive sniffing of markers.

"I like the smell of the red ones the best, but green is good too. If you smell them both together it smells like Watermelon Bubbleyum. Is your name Punk?"

The boys eyed each other cautiously. A baseball cap was mashed onto Brad's head. He had a dirty face and scraped knees, hands covered in marker. He had a mouth stained with juice. This was what a cool person looked like. This was who Punk wanted to drink juice with.

"Yeah. My name is Punk. I only have black and brown markers."

Brad handed Punk the red and green in exchange for the black and brown.

"I'll smell those for awhile. The red and green are making me dizzy. I like punk rock music. Is that why your name is Punk? Because you like punk rock music? Your parents must be cool. You must be cool."

Punk had never heard of such a thing as punk rock music before. However, it became abundantly clear that his new friend was an arbiter of style and fashion. Punk did not wish to appear foolish.

"Yes. I like punk rock music. Do you like skateboarding?"

"Yeah, skateboarding is cool. I can do a kickflip," replied Brad. This was a lie, he could not do a kick flip, but it was clear to him that his new friend was far more interesting and athletic than he. The only word that Brad had ever heard, related to skateboarding was the word "kickflip" so he used it.

Twenty years later, Peter was Punk. Peter was dead. Punk was dead, too, but not as dead as Peter. Brad was still Brad, and he wondered most evenings how close to alive he was.

Brad stayed up most nights, listening to The Misfits. He sat alone in his studio apartment, looking out the window and taking rips off his bong thinking about their first conversation and waiting to speak with his best friend again. Most nights the memories made him smile. Some nights he wished they had never met. Other nights he wondered if he lost his mind every year on the night of Punk's death. On those nights, he would lose himself in a deep aromatic cloud of herb, as he watched the traffic out the window. When his girlfriend stayed over, she bothered him about how much pot he smoked, usually while smoking with him. She would pass out, a pile of limbs and hair and he would be alone again, watching the traffic grind lazily into the night. He wondered how he got here. He counted the days until he would see Punk again. On those nights he drifted off to dreamless sleep he hoped that the dead boy was just a part of his deranged imagination.

4

22 Hours Remaining

They skated until they reached the Redondo Beach Pier. Brad's shirt dripped with sweat even in the December cold. Punk did not sweat. They skated hard because it was better than talking. The pot and the booze melted the corners off of everything. When they walked on the concrete of the pier they could still feel the movement of the boards under their feet. They owned everything around them. The Mexican families fishing off over the side of the pier, the sailors swilling beer in bayside bars, and the maniacally grinning clown mural on the wall of the Fun Factory Arcade all belonged to them. They were infinite. They were giants. They were perfectly drunk and high.

They stumbled, skateboards slung over shoulders down the center of the main drag of the pier. Brad slapped a man selling light-up pinwheels a loud and perfect high-five. Punk impressed some high school girls on his skateboard. They asked him if he had a Facebook account. He told them *no*. They said that was cool and wondered aloud what high school he went to. Brad cracked up, grabbed Punk, knocked his hood off, and gave him a ferocious noogie. The girls took another look at Punk in the fluorescent lights of the pier. Their faces dropped when they saw him completely. They turned on a dime and walked away. Brad heard one of them say;

"I think he's got some weird, like, disease or something. Don't stare."

Brad slapped Punk on the back and pulled the hood back over his head. They played video games at the arcade. They ate churros. They flirted with drunken elderly women hanging out of the windows of bars. Then they heard it. The first chords of Danzig's Mother ripped through the air. They followed the sound to a middle-aged cover band shredding the song like they were playing for an audience of a thousand screaming fans rather then forty aging punks.

Brad and Punk threw their boards down in the bar and jumped into the mosh pit. They pushed and punched in the melee. They slammed their heads forward throwing sprays of sweat into the already drenched backs of the other punks. They were together in their rage at some unknowable phantom that had stolen something from them. They punched and fought with the air because their real enemy was nowhere to be seen. Punk threw his hood back, shut his eyes, and began throwing fists and elbows and knees and feet to the music. Faster. Louder. He wanted more and more. He wanted everything but the desert at the bottom of the ocean. He wanted to fuck something up. One of his cold fists connected with a square jaw in the mosh pit.

"What the hell!" A barrel chested forty-something with the thousand yard stare of a sailor rubbed his jaw. The sailor's eyes bore into Punk. The dead boy stared right back. The man glared back at Punk, the frozen time between match and fuse. Something in Punk's eyes quenched the fire in the man's chest.

"What's your problem, man?" asked Punk, nose to nose with the man even though he was a head shorter.

"Are you sick or something?"

"What? You've never seen a dead body before?" Punk asked. He coughed and then spat salt water and whiskey onto the man's shirt. A thin string of seaweed hung out the side of his mouth.

Punk felt strong hands on his sweatshirt and he was lifted off his feet and thrown to the beer-drenched floor. Punk rebounded, bulldogging the sailor in the gut. No one in the pit noticed the fight. Arms clasped around

Punk's waist. He drew back a pale fist and punched the man in the groin. The guy doubled over for a second and Punk let his guard drop. A smile flicked onto his china doll face. He waited for the guy to get back on his feet. He wanted to feel the fist against his face. He wanted warm blood to flow from him rather than cold salt water. He wanted to feel something break inside of him.

Hit me. Hit me. Hit me.

The Sailor charged him, cocking back a crushing fist. Punk waited for annihilation. The guy fell on his ass as Brad swept the feet out from under him with his skateboard. The edge of the board connected with the man's shins. It sound like a baseball being smacked over the far fence. The mosh pit swirled around them. The sailor tried to push himself back onto his feet when a brand new Airwalk skate shoe collapsed his cheek. The lead singer of the band screamed in time with the crescendo of guitars. Brad and Punk kicked the man, and no one could hear the impact from the shoes or the yelps of pain from the sailor. The Mosh pit swirled. The man screamed.

5

"If you move fast enough you won't get burned!" Punk yelled from the end of the block.

"Watch!"

Brad sat on his skateboard, rolling from side to side. He sucked on a watermelon *Jolly Rancher*. A fire made of dried branches, leaves and newspapers crackled in the middle of the street in between two ramps made of cinder blocks and plywood.

Punk positioned himself at the entrance of the cul-de-sac. He lined up his skateboard with the ramp and squatted down to lower his center of gravity on the board. Brad crunched through his *Jolly Rancher* and reached into his pocket to replace it with another watermelon flavored *Jolly Rancher*. Punk raced towards the makeshift ramp. He was the smallest in his 5th grade class. He was always the smallest, but when he was on his skateboard he was a million miles tall. There wasn't a gap he couldn't be dared to jump. He would grind the same rail for hours. Most nights he came home with a pair of bleeding wrists from wiping out, and a torn knees from picking himself back up.

The tail of the board hit the apex of the ramp at the perfect time to send him sailing across the small gap, over the fire, and onto other side. He burned out his board in front of Brad.

"Now you try."

Brad choked down his fresh *Jolly Rancher*.

"I don't want to." Brad counted the white flecks in the asphalt at his feet.

"But it's a dare. You dared me, now I dare you."

"I don't want to though." Brad looked at the smoldering branches in between the plywood ramps.

"It's easy. You just have to go really fast. Just go really fast. I dare you. Now you have to do it."

Punk looked down at Brad, his board slung over his shoulder. The dare was a shot across the bow. It was a test, a fictional dare, like try and steal a cop's gun or touch a girl's boob. Brad never believed that Punk would do it. Brad hoped that a police officer or a parent would happen upon them and tell them to put the fire out. None did.

"I did it. You have to do it," Punk said.

Brad pushed his board to the edge of the cul-de-sac on his own green mile. He lined up his board with the small pillar of smoke billowing from in between the ramps. He pushed off.

Punk did it, so I can do it. Punk did it, so I can do it. Punk did it, so I can do it.

The sound of the wheels and the crackling of the fire was all Brad could hear. The trucks of the board smacked into the ramp. Brad went head first into the flames. He was proud of his scars for months

6

Clack Clack!

Their boards hit the pavement outside of the bar. They pumped as hard as they could, assuming the guy would have been up and after them in seconds if Brad hadn't broken the dude's legs. Brad followed along a winding path in between the office park on the pier. They were alone in a secluded corner of the boardwalk. Punk pulled up his hood and looked over the bay gazing off at the blinking red light on the breakwater.

Brad stopped his board a couple feet behind Punk. He did not want to be at this part of the pier.

"Why'd you lead us here?" he asked, taking a slug off of the bottle.

"I just wanted to look at it. Be back here tomorrow night huh?" Brad couldn't see Punk's face, but he could hear a smile in his voice.

The rail was perfect. A five set of stairs and a miraculously smooth handrail. Enough space to land and catch speed down the incline to hop a gap between two benches. It was the kind of rail that made skaters drool. The drop into the black churning sea down below, made it better. The fear heightened the senses, and sharpened everything. If someone had the balls to land it and complete the set, they were legend.

"I want to go. Let's go. That guy might find us," said Brad.

"No one is going to find us."

"What's wrong with you tonight?"

Punk stood swaying back and forth ever so slightly. His black hooded form outlined by the blinking red light at the end of the breakwater. He spat up a little seawater.

"I'm... I'm just sick of being down there. It's so cold. It's dark. It's always dark. and there is no one. Nothing down there. Can't hear a thing, can't see a thing. You can just remember. I just want something more to remember. You know?"

"Man... I... I'm..." Something clutched in Brad's belly. His voice quivered and he stopped.

"It's okay."

Punk thought about the sound of the board snapping in two. He felt weightlessness. He felt time become invalid. Then the tug of gravity. He fell for an eternity. He was swallowed up by the icy water. He dropped like a rock beneath the black/green waves. He remembered looking up and seeing the lights of fishing boats shining down into the ocean to attract their prey. They looked like stars in the night sky. Then he let his final lung full of air go.

"I'm sorry," Brad croaked, his head buried between his knees as he rolled back and forth on his board.

"I know," said Punk's silhouette in the blinking red light.

Brad said nothing he just rolled gently from side to side.

Punk turned to him with a forced smile plastered on his blue lips.

"I'm sorry, man. I'm just fucked up right now. Let's get out of here."

Punk laid his board down and skated off trailing the smell of the sea. Brad looked at the railing gleaming in the moonlight. He put his board on the railing and slid it along, listening to the scrape of the wood on ring on the steel.

They slept in Brad's car that night.

Punk wouldn't sleep though. He couldn't. He had stayed awake for years in consuming nothingness. He didn't know if it was hell, or purgatory, or prison. It just was. He wondered if anyone who ever died was under the ground, waiting for what was next, slowly trying to forget about their life.

He was awake when Brad nodded off into a deep snore. He was awake when the sun began to sail high into the air. He watched the glittering top of the water and marveled at how cold it could be at the bottom.

5

12 Hours Remaining.

"So there was all of these people protesting, and they camped out in front of city hall for like a month. I went down to see the freak show or whatever. I don't know, it's over now. Terrorists and shit are still, like, everywhere. Some days I'm like, well, I'm going to get killed by a terrorist. Like, that is just how I'm going to go." Brad stopped himself because he didn't like talking about dying in front of Punk. It was awkward.

"Shit. What else happened this year?" Brad asked to no one in particular sitting in the driver's seat of his Toyota Echo, idling at a stop light on the corner of Hollywood Boulevard and Vine. A cold joint hung out of the corner of his mouth. He removed it to take a slug of 5-hour energy because he knew that he had to be completely alert and awake for the next 12 hours. That much he owed to his friend. The couple of hours sleep in his car had done nothing. It was all the time his best friend had on the anniversary of the day that he died. Brad wasn't going to let it go to waste. Punk flipped through radio stations, one after another trying to find a song that he recognized. He brought the smell of seaweed and salt into the car with him.

"What did we do last year? Shit, has it really already been a year? That's insane! Do you realize how insane that is? Punk! A year has passed." Punk looked up from the radio and pulled his hood back from his eyes.

Brad was startled to see them in the light. They had gone milky and reflective. They blended into his pale cheeks.

"I don't know. I don't remember much from last year. What movie did we see?"

"Batman. I think it was Batman."

The light turned green and they fell silent. Brad stepped on the gas, took the joint from the corner of his mouth, and handed it to Punk.

"Do you want to start this up again?"

"I'll wait on it."

Brad nodded. Silence hung heavy in the car, along with the smell of weed and salt. Brad wanted to ask Punk how his year was. Brad wanted Punk to grow up and get taller.

"Do you see my mom at all?" Punk asked. A small dagger pierced Brad's heart.

"Nah, man. I mean, I used to call her or whatever. but I don't know. We're not in the same neighborhood any more. My folks kind of kicked me out because of stuff with Sharon. That's my girlfriend. I don't know if you remember her or whatever. It's pretty hard to get down to Redondo Beach to say hey to your mom, but this year totally. I'll be better about it. I'm trying to be like, better about everything. This year…"

"But you're going to see her right?" Punk asked, turning his dead eyes back to Brad.

"Yeah, man, of course. Yeah, I thought that I'd do that day after tomorrow. Tonight, there is this stupid vampire angel war movie that's out. It looks completely retarded, so I suggest that we get super baked and see this thing. It's at the cheap theater too, so it's on me."

"Cool. Hey, thanks for the clothes and stuff, man."

"Yeah, dude, of course."

"Will you come back to the ocean with me tonight?"

Brad paused.

He finished off his Five-Hour Energy. The thought of Punk falling over the railing of the pier again was almost too much for him to bear. He saw his friend's slight form being swallowed by the sea, and the Black Flag logo on his sweatshirt disappearing into the cold water. Brad pushed that thought out of his head just like he did every day when his mind was quiet for a moment.

"I don't know. We'll see if work calls me or not. They're total dicks this time of year because no one is coming in- because it's cold."

"Yeah, it's cold. I mean just to like hang out until we… well, until midnight. You know? It would be great to have you there."

"Yeah, dude. I want to. Just, work and stuff."

"I understand."

Punk found a station playing Bad Religion's *21st Century Digital Boy*.

The first chords rattled the car's cheap speakers. Brad rolled down all of the windows. Without a glance towards one another they began screaming out the lyrics. Brad laid on the gas pedal. The lights, and the soot, and the beautiful, and the ugly of Hollywood Boulevard melted into one grimy red fluorescent blur.

4

Brad held the pipe for Punk. He couldn't quite figure out how to cover the carb with his thumb and light the bowl at the same time. The summer was drawing to a close and their senior year of high school was looming like a mushroom cloud on the horizon. Summer nights by the ocean were a special kind of California perfect. They lay back on a sand dune under the pier. Barnacle encrusted pylons sunk deep into the ocean supported the boardwalk. Brad would take a hit and then lean over to hold the pipe and light the bowl for Punk.

Punk took a decent rip off the pipe and fell back into a coughing fit in the sand. Brad didn't laugh. He just smiled and looked up at the underside of the pier and mumbled:

"You don't cough, you don't get off, man."

Eyes bloodshot in his black hood, a loose giggle bubbled from deep in Punk's sweatshirt. Brad took out his Diskman CD player and a couple of makeshift speakers. He set them in the sand, being careful to make sure that none got in the Diskman. He took out a burned CD with a masking tape label that read, *Ignite*. He pressed play. A cover of *Sunday Bloody Sunday* played, echoing off of the boards of the pier.

"I have no idea what this song is about, but I like it. I like it a lot. It, like... it's good." Brad laughed at the nonsense that Punk was talking. He had only just started smoking. Every time he smoked he would talk nonsense for hours, eat his parents entire fridge, and then claim the next day not to have felt anything.

"You're stoned, man. Listen to it later. It's good."

"I'm not stoned. I'm telling you, dude, this stuff doesn't work on me."

"Bullshit." Brad balked.

"What? No, I could totally, like, drive a car or something. I don't see what you get out of this. Are those cops up there?"

A pair of headlights passed over the pier.

"We're fine, dude. You don't have a car or a license. So you couldn't drive any way."

"I could skate. I'd be totally okay." A bad idea rose like a demon in Brad's mind. It became a smile on his face.

"Alright, Punk. Then I have a dare for you." Punk rolled over in the sand, his eyes bloodshot to hell.

"Shoot my friend."

"Grind the rail."

"The rail?"

"Yeah. I dare you."

The words rang like a bell in the air. Punk rolled back over and looked up at the underside of the pier.

"Brad. Pack up your shit. Get your board."

4

8 hours Remaining.

"So I think that Sharon is pregnant."

Brad exhaled slowly through his nose and clenched his jaw. Punk said nothing, he just looked out the window at the passing life.

"But, I don't know. Like, she lies about stuff some times. She told me about her brother for, like, months. Then, I found out that she didn't have a brother. I don't know. She said, "I might be pregnant," before she went to go and see her family in Northern California. I mean, that's a messed up way of telling me, so now I'm like: What the fuck? You know? No text, no call, nothing. You know?"

Punk kept his hood over his eyes, the words washing meaninglessly over him. The street was singing to him. The bottom of the deep oceanic trench where he died was an expanse of nothingness with an occasional vent on the ocean floor spitting bubbles from one abyss to another. It was nothing but a frigid black void.

"I mean, I don't even know why I live here. I'm, like a bartender, which I can do anywhere. And I was thinking about…"

Punk's milky eyes followed an immaculate woman in a white dress down the street. She smiled sadly and carried bag full of clinking wine bottles. She made eye contact with everyone she walked past on the street. Punk averted his eyes under his hood. He didn't want to scare her. She looked so clean. A prostitute in a short blonde bob strutted by him on six-inch spike heels, a car horn cried, and the sky bruised to a dark indigo.

"So, I was thinking about leaving."

The sentence snapped Punk's attention back to Brad who chewed the end of a blunt until a thin stream of black liquid began to roll down his chin.

"What?" asked Punk

"Like, leaving Los Angeles. Going, maybe to Northern California with Sharon. Like, I mean, if she *is* pregnant or something. I don't know." Brad sparked the blunt and puffed it until his face was lit in the cinders. "I guess what I'm saying is…"

"You're not going to come and see me any more."

Punk watched a man in a black coat walking across the street. The man had a gasoline can and seemed to be humming to himself. Punk liked that man. Brad handed the blunt to Punk who burned the tip to ashes, sucking until every last burning cinder of pot fell deep into his chest. He could almost hear the hiss as the cinders burnt out in the saltwater in his lungs.

"Let's go to a movie. You want to go to a movie?" Brad looked concerned. He had said it. Now it was impossible to take back. You can't take words back. He would carry this dead boy with him everywhere he went.

"Yeah, let's get out of here," Punk said, taking out his pipe and packing a bowl. He saw the man with the gas can walking in the distance and part of him wanted to go with that man. He wanted to see something combust.

5

6 Hours Remaining.

The movie theatre seats creaked under their weight as they collapsed into them. Their eyes were sunset-red and their voices were burned ragged. Since their conversation on Hollywood Boulevard they hadn't said a word to one another. They packed the pipe, smoked it down, and packed another. Numb from the inside out, they could undergo dental surgery and not even flinch.

Punk turned around in his seat. The preshow muzik hummed annoyingly as Brad giggled at the screen which was twisting and morphing as the projectionist tried to get the frame right. Punk watched a couple in the back row. She was feeding him chocolate. He winced at the taste, but he smiled for her. A drunk woman in white stumbled in and took a seat on the side. Try as she might, she could barely keep herself upright. She slouched back and her head lolled to the left.

He wondered what these people were doing tonight. He wondered what lives they were leaving for a moment to be lost between the frames of the film. He wondered what lives they would go back to.

"Yo, dude. There's a fucking baby in here." Brad pointed to a kid in the front row. Punk laughed.

"Cheap movie theater. They let ANYONE in here!" Brad went on. He turned his bloodshot gaze to Punk and did his best impression of sobriety. "Hey, man, listen." Punk didn't turn his head to Brad. He looked straight towards the flickering screen, trying to find meaning in the projectionist's mistakes. Only his lips and nose were visible out of his hood. The lights began to lower.

"About what I said earlier. Seriously, I'm not going to… I mean, I'm not going to fucking… *leave* you. Like, I wouldn't *leave you* alone."

An usher with an artificial voice box walked to the front of the screen. He told everyone to enjoy the show. The lights dimmed. The opening credits of the movie began to play.

"But IF- and that is a big IF," Brad went on talking over the opening music of the film. An angel flew onto the screen. "IF I go… I just want you to know…"

Punk grabbed Brad's arm with his cold dead hand. He stopped talking immediately.

"Shut. Up. You do whatever you want. Okay? You have my blessing or whatever." Punk turned to look at Brad. The pearlescent whites of his eyes were made paler by the flickering of the movie screen. He pulled a broad false smile over his face.

"But…" Punk leaned in and whispered in Brad's ear and the dead boy's lips were close enough for Brad to feel the ice on his neck.

"You come back to the pier with me tonight…" Punk leaned in closer.

The soundtrack of the movie filled the auditorium and Brad stared blankly at the screen. Someone in the back was row was crying. The intoxication of the weed had been bleached from his system. Brad was stone cold sober. He sat straight as an arrow in his seat. He didn't hear a single word of the movie or anything else after Punk said:

"I dare you."

6

1 Hour remaining.

The boards rattled against one another in the back seat of Brad's car. He could hear the ball bearings shaking the wheels of his board. He was silent. They both were. The 101 freeway bled into the 110 and then the 105 until they hit the beach in El Segundo. They drove along the water and Brad could not help but steal glances at the heaving frigid ocean. He couldn't help but glance down at the thin almost translucent skin pulled taut and thin across Punk's hand.

He replayed every bit of Punk's last leap in his head. The placement of the board on the rail. The distance that he ollied from. The side of the rail that he put his weight on. The depth of his crouch.

Punk was a better skater than Brad and they both knew it. They knew the odds of Brad grinding the rail and then completing the session by jumping the gap was nearly impossible. Brad had nightmares that he was riding towards the rail, speeding towards it, too fast or too slow. He saw himself falling head first into the blackness of the ocean churning below. Sometimes he fell straight down. Sometimes his head caught one of the barnacle covered pylons as he came down. Even in his dreams it was impossible. His foot was shaking as he pushed the emergency brake on.

"Let's go. You don't have much time." Without another word, Brad and Punk grabbed their skateboards from the trunk. Normally, they would skate to the rail, but they walked. Brad was grateful that they were walking. His legs were shaking so badly that he could barely stand on his board. He put a joint between his lips then thought better of it and tucked it behind his ear.

They exited the parking structure only to be smacked in the face by a fierce winter wind off of the ocean. If they leaned into the wind they might be able to be supported on nothing but the breeze holding them up. It twisted and blew with an intelligence all it's own, as if it could choose to push one way or pull another in a heartbeat.

Brad looked over to Punk. He was leaning into the wind the loose ends of his baggy sweatshirt flapping in the heavy draft. His hood had blown off. Punk loved feeling the dry salty wind across his body. He loved feeling as if he may begin to fly at a moment's notice. He wanted to burn the memory of the night sky and the stars into his mind. He walked to the edge running his hand along the metal railing and turned to Brad.

Brad dropped his board to the pavement with a *clack*. He put his foot on the grip tape. The trucks wobbled slightly with the shaking of his foot. He spotted his session. Ollie the five set. Don't over shoot the rail. Stick it and boardslide the curve. Pop off, get speed down the ramp and hop the final gap. Burn out to stop for extra style. But this wasn't about style.

Punk turned to him, backlit in the rhythmically flashing red light at the end of the breakwater. Even in the shadow of his sweatshirt and the midnight black of the ocean, Brad could make out his pale face hovering in the depths of his hood.

"You sure you want to do this?" The wind carried Punk's voice in a way that made it sound like it came from every direction.

"Get out of the way."

Brad rolled his board forward and back trying to read the break of the pavement in front of him. Punk moved off to the side. As he watched Brad's knee shake, he wanted to call it off and let them both go home. But he knew the politics of the dare. He knew that the stakes riding on it had grown too great. This would end tonight. Part of him wanted nothing more than to see his best friend go over into the darkness.

Brad sucked air and prepared to launch himself towards the ocean. The wind pushed against his chest and then grabbed his shirt, and pulled him forward. It tossed him to the side and pushed him off of his feet again. He stood for one frozen second trying to will his limbs to life. He only had minutes until the sea took

Punk back. He decided that he would never come back here ever again after this night.

He gritted his teeth.

He pushed.

Before he knew it he was twisting the trunk of his body, and pumping his arms as his heel dug into the concrete. Punk became a shadowy blur in his periphery. He could feel every grain and imperfection in the concrete of the pier. The board began a small speed wobble. Brad lowered his center of gravity to compensate. The only thing that existed to him was the rail. The slick curve of it shined in the moonlight. The edge of the stairs approached quicker than he thought.

He slapped the tail of his board, just catching the last couple inches of stair. The top of his shoe slid up the rough grip tape as he evened out mid-air. The wind felt like a rough hand on the back of his neck pulling him into the ocean. The expanse of the black ocean opened before him like a hungry mouth, and he felt himself going into it.

Clack!

The board caught. Dead center. It balanced between the trucks, the rail making a tenuous fulcrum between the concrete and the ocean. He flew around the curve, feeling every smooth inch of metal railing under his feet. The wind teeter-tottered him from side to side. One side concrete and maybe some road rash, the other side, icy oblivion.

The end of the curve came too quickly leaving him no room to dismount properly. He twisted his body mid air and felt himself going backwards over the rail. He caught a glimpse of the barnacle-covered pylons. He thought he saw Punk lying, floating in the water, gazing up at him.

Brad twisted back, and came shooting off of the rail. His board slapped on the ground. The wind pushed him down the incline. Something deep and cold uncoiled in his gut, he would make it. He wanted more. He wanted more wind, more speed, more danger. More, more, more. He pushed harder and harder, until the final gap approached. When the tail of the board smacked into the pavement, and he dragged his shoe against the grip tape, he felt himself in flight. He hung in the air, motionless in velocity. Everything turned to ashes. His shitty job, his pregnant girlfriend, his disappointed parents. It was all meaningless in this blissful inertia.

He never wanted to come down.

When the wheels touched the ground and scraped to a halt. Brad whirled around on his back two wheels, ecstatic laughter pouring from his mouth into the senseless night wind. He looked for his friend to share the moment with.

As he turned, he caught sight of Punk's fresh shoes going over the edge, plummeting down into the water. And he was gone. Gone again for another year. He left nothing but Brad standing there. His board was wedged between the concrete of the pier and the rubber of his shoe.

Brad caught his breath. He kicked the board into his hand, the cool metal of the trucks slid into his sweating palm. He walked towards the edge. He put his hands on the railing and looked down into the blackness of the ocean. At this time of night, it was indistinguishable from the sky.

He lit a joint. Across the pier he could hear the people laughing and the clinking of glasses. There were colored lights and drunken karaoke. There were families shucking the shells off of oysters and lovers sharing a kiss with December cold lips. There were people finishing their last lonely drink of the night. Brad picked up his board and turned it over. He looked at the deep scar left where the railing had bitten into the wood. The deep cut in the board was proof. *Punk is not dead, he's just waiting. He's breathing cold water in salty lungs, and watching the surface of the water,* thought Brad.

Brad left his skateboard floating in the ink black sea. Slowly, it was pulled to the bottom.

L.A. History 3

The Abridged Corrected History of Los Angeles
"Gangland Steer Hands"
1849-1911

With the Gold Rush in full swing in Northern California, the American Association of Freemasons began surveying the rivers and valleys of the Los Angeles River Basin for fistfuls of gold dust and the god-like power of wealth in a poor land. They dredged the river and sifted the rocky soil to gather the demonic gold at the bottom of it. The gold was then forged by blind craftsmen into the figure of an owl representing the pagan god, Baal. This owl sits underneath the Walt Disney Concert Hall at 111 South Grand Avenue. It is still worshipped today. The Masons made sacrifices to the golden owl that it may bring prosperity and dark power to the Los Angeles River Basin. They pulled still-beating hearts from the chests of screaming Mexican natives and placed the steaming entrails on the altar of Baal. The soothsayers read the entrails and were horrified to realize the true destiny of this nexus between apocalypse and infinity. "Cows!" moaned the seer. "Cows!" With that, his spirit left him, in a rictus of ecstatic joy and the terror of the pit.

Queen of the Cowtowns

Fat wild cows began pouring into the Los Angeles River Basin. Wide-eyed, lowing, thick with meat, and heavy with milk, they streamed into the city leaving the cleverest amongst the American settlers and the most daring of the Native Mexicans to capitalize on the beef trade. While the Gold Rush in San Francisco attracted the attention of the rest of the United States, Los Angeles set its sights on the meat trade. Enormous stinking herds of cattle grew like tumors across the land. The herds of Los Angeles dwarfed those in the rest of California. So much so that an entire economy sprung from the cows' nutrient rich feces. Dung lords and fertilizer kings lined their pockets with the profits of stinking gold. The smell of manure and meat filled the streets of Los Angeles giving it the new nickname, "Queen of the Cowtowns." All praise be to Baal and the golden owl for a city built upon bullshit and meat.

American ranch hands and cowboys fresh off of the Mexican-American War journeyed across the American west to homestead in Los Angeles, hoping to make their living off of the backs of steers. However, given the transition between Mexican and American governments, the city entered into a period of abject lawlessness. American cowboys shot down Mexican vampires in the streets, while aboriginals lured the children of Freemasons from their cribs appearing in the form of adorable animals. Ethiopian slaves called up dead ranchers to perform their bidding and Spanish monks still tattooed the teachings of the bible on their own backs.

The constitution of California was being rewritten again in blood and meat and shit. God and Satan no longer vied for control, neither one wanted it. They watched it carefully as one would a soap opera or a helicopter crash.

The Death of a Ranch Hand

No political system or dogma could seal the growing divide between the old world and the new. Racial, spiritual, ethical, political, and supernatural tensions all came to a head in 1855 with the wealth from the cattle drives fanning the flames of revolution.

A letter from ranch hand Josie Avett describes the mood of anarchy in Los Angeles:

"Mother,
There is a murder a day in Los Angeles. Strange cries and moans break the air nightly. They are silenced only by gunfire. Though I have seen battle in the West, I am afraid each night of the silence in between the shrieks. Something has been killing the cattle and draining them of all their blood. It is like nothing I have ever seen on a ranch. I am told that if I find the creature and kill it, I will never want for gold. I will hunt the creature if only to return home to you, Edgar, and the twins. Tell Father that I will turn my back on this reeking town with gold in my pocket and the future in my eye..."

-Josie

Josie Avett was found drained of all his blood, the letter clutched in his cold dead fingers. The death of Josie Avett was blamed on Mexican gangs and inflamed racial tensions. The golden owl of the Freemasons demanded tribute and incited a kind of madness that seized the hearts of the people. Vigilante committees were formed to troll for Mexican blood under the guise of avenging the death of Josie Avett. Sadly, the myopic unschooled farm hands could not recognize the telltale signs of mass possession combined with a simple Chupacabra attack. Had they made even the slightest inquiry into the death of this young farmhand many lives would have been spared.

The Saint of Bandits

The vigilante committees began rounding up Mexican vaqueros and convicting them in kangaroo courts. The charges ranged from cattle rustling to fornication with demons. Oddly, both charges held the same sentence: death by hanging. These killings uncapped the inherent Mexican nationalism in the native population of Los Angeles. They implored God to intercede on their behalf. They burned ceremonial fires to Toypurina and threw offerings to The Great and Terrible Sea Monster. Their prayers were answered by Juan Flores, or "The Saint of Bandits" as he came to be known.

Juan Flores led a gang of insurrectionists called "Las Manillas" or "The Handcuffs" in a rebellion against the American oppressors. Flores led a series of raids and robberies targeted at returning Southern California to the Mexican people. His gun was forged from the wings of fallen angels, his vest was the tanned hide of a pit demon, and his bullets were regular bullets, but he was extremely good at shooting them. He was said to have the Lord's Prayer always on his lips in the midst of the fiercest gun battles and his lead always found the heart of a gringo.

The cabal of Grand Master Masons who lived in Spanish style mansions at the center of Pershing Square watched as their cattle and their cow hands scared from the fields by a growing folk legend. They consulted their golden owl idol who offered a disinterested shrug to The Freemasons. They offered Flores gold to stop his campaign of destruction. When the Saint of Bandits refused they decided in a typical Angelino fashion that it would be best to kill him. In Los Angeles, it is always best to ignore a problem until it goes away; if that doesn't work, attempt to buy the problem, if that doesn't work, wage absolute war on it. When none of that works, submit to the problem entirely and become a part of it.

The Masons hired raiding parties of Texas Rangers to track The Saint of Bandits. They were renown for their superior tracking skills, Christian values, and abject racism and therefore were perfect to find the insurrectionist. They drove their horses hard and fast out into the desert, making sure that Flores was nowhere near a Catholic church from which he drew his power. He was chased deep into the desert. The Desert of Southern California is one of the few known places where God cannot hear or see you.

Flores was surrounded by Rangers when his horse could go no further. He died in a hail of bullets, The Lord's Prayer was still on his lips. Before he lay dead in the sand he killed seventeen Texas Rangers with only eight bullets. Out of respect for the Saint of Bandits, they brought his body to a church on the outskirts of the city. He was given his last rites by a Mexican Padre which prompted him to return from the dead, reload his gun and take out six more Texas Rangers crying:

"Viva Mexico! Viva Los Insurrectos! Viva Las Manilias! Nosotros La Gente-"

Sick of his inspiring rhetoric, the remaining Texas Rangers decided to hang him from a tree branch and wait until birds of prey had eaten away all but a skeleton of the Saint of Bandits. His skeleton was recently recovered during the construction of a water feature in Echo Park. The skeleton stalks through Echo Park and Silver Lake late at night attempting to unseat the American invaders.

Cattletown Shakedown

The wealth from the herds of cattle, their subsequent by-products, and the low boiling gold rush put California at the center of American crosshairs. People went where the money was, and the railroads went where the people went and Los Angeles made its mark on the American identity. Enraptured by the idea that great wealth goes to those who do not fear death or un-death was enough to capture the imagination of legions of American settlers. The population surged from only a couple thousand in the 1870s to over a hundred thousand human residents in the early 1900s. It should be noted that supernatural residents were already numbering well in the millions as many need neither railroads to move, nor food to eat.

Iron Horse

America in the early 1870s was being girdled by iron and railroad ties and Chinese laborers were the muscle and know-how behind the iron horse of the 1900s. Along with the railroads came Korean and Japanese farmers. Each ethnic group establishing cultural enclaves around the city. They brought with them language, religions, and certain curses. Each group eyed the other warily, each group claimed the city as their own. When the ground would rumble a tremor or get washed out by a flood they would pray for the destruction of the others. A wary peace was born at the end of the 1900s.

    Perhaps it was the rumbling steam engines or the coal smoke belching into the perfect blue California sky. The powers that govern the netherworld around Los Angeles decided that things were far too comfortable. God and Satan returned to their age-old experiment. They dried up the water and they rained down gold. Los Angeles got thirsty and rich. Then and only then did a hundred thousand Angelinos realize that they were lured into a desert by a mirage"

The Vampire Andy

Saturday morning came. I was watching an infomercial in Spanish, and I was thinking about bursting into flame. The English guy dubbed in Spanish blended marinara. My eyelashes lit like birthday candles. He chopped garlic with ease. The skin around my smiling mouth blackened and flaked. He sliced. I singed. He diced. I seared. He pureed. I disappeared into white flame. Finally. I couldn't sleep since she left, so I sat on my couch and detested the world.

I hated Saturday mornings. Farmers market day in West Hollywood, an orgy of ego drenched self satisfied hipsters fondling tomatoes and dirty talking one another about their shrinking carbon footprints. The thought of food made me sick. I had eaten too much that night. I could feel my stomach beginning to roll over my jeans. I was glad I didn't have a mirror. I got mean when I didn't sleep. I never slept anymore. I was mean this morning for no other reason than my favorite infomercial was in Spanish.

Six A.M. sapphire blue light seeped through the venetian blinds. The light told me that I should have been asleep long ago. I could hear Mexican day laborers unloading crates of microgreens and kale to be setup in booths by their trust fund subsidized, proto-hippy, grad school drop out bosses. I loved hating them so much that I was almost happy for another bout of sleeplessness. I hopped off the couch and got my window stick to get a better look.

The window stick was an insomnia inspired invention. It sat in the corner of my studio next to the television. The window stick was an old shower curtain rod with a radio antenna duct taped to it. I pulled it from its home wedged in a pile of tacky platform pumps with spike heels that I had been meaning to throw out, but they just kept accumulating like so many fast food containers.

I extended the antenna on top of the window stick and perched myself in the shade of the room straddling my couch. Extending the window stick with surgical accuracy I drew down a peephole in my Venetian blinds. Sunlight spilled onto the chrome of the antennae and glinted painfully in my eye. The sun was already higher than I imagined. Was it summer or fall? It doesn't matter in L.A. A couple less hours of perfect sunny days didn't make much difference to me. The golden rays pooled on the floor between the window and my couch.

The market was drenched in the blush of the early west coast sun. The white nylon tents sat in an orderly row with twenty-something couples strolling in the dreamlike state of new romance, cyclists sipping lattes congregating in a makeshift café, and vendors giving out generous samples of bulging exotic fruits. The food looked like ash. The smiling couples hurt me like the glint of sun in my eye. A bubble of deep regret floated along my spine, and something seized in my stomach. The blinds rattled as I withdrew the stick. The bubble burst somewhere near my heart and an angry sorrow lit up my chest. I bit my hand to keep my spider webbing insides intact.

Unable to stop myself, I recalled a dizzying montage of memories. Her platinum blonde bob. Her. The neon lights on Sunset spotlighting her on the street corner. Her. The smell of iron and melting sugar as she got into my car the first time. Her, her, her. The low pull of her moan. The eyes. The hands. Those teeth. Those teeth. Everything changed with those teeth. Alabaster. Perfect alabaster white.

The memories burst a dam of rage inside of me. I threw the stick onto the floor in the pool of sunlight and leapt off my couch. I squeezed my eyes and bit my hand harder. The pain from my teeth was nothing compared to the universe of hurt in my gut. I wanted to destroy something beautiful and sweet. I wanted to kick holes in the walls. I wanted to ignite. I wanted to cause someone as much pain as I felt.

Instead, I decided to eat.

I ran a hand along my softening stomach. Tomorrow I start my diet. I thought. I removed my mouth from my hand. Two neat holes. No blood.

I went to the bathroom. Before I opened the door I tried to convince myself to chew a piece of gum instead, the saliva pooling in my mouth convinced me otherwise. I placed my head on the door with a gentle thunk and thought, 'Am I hungry?' Then, 'No I'm just depressed.' I opened the door to the bathroom. The girl was lying in the bathtub where I left her.

A stream of blood ran down her neck and out of her thin wrists; it formed a shallow pool at the bottom of the tub. Her legs were like pale sticks. Her platform shoes with nine inch spikes were thrown in the corner. Her eyes lazily rotated in their orbits toward me. Even below her thick red lipstick, her lips seemed blue. Her hair was chopped, short and blonde. While I had my mouth around her neck I could pretend for a bit.

I stood in the doorway feeling self-conscious. I didn't think she would still be awake and I was already coming back for a fourth helping. It was like that moment when I still ate food, where I wanted to take the last slice of pizza. I never did because I would have been embarrassed. If left to my own devices I would have devoured the pizza entirely. It was like that. This time the pizza was watching me. And judging me.

"Are you going to kill me?" she croaked, as if she were asking the time. She'd lost so much blood she was punch drunk.

"Yes," I said guiltily. Conscious of my gut.

"Oh." Her eyes returned to their previous position fixed on something on the far wall.

"Do I look fat to you?"

The question jumped out of my mouth. I wanted to cram the words back in but they already hung in the air and glowed in self conscious neon. Her eyes rotated slowly back to me again. I felt naked, but I pushed my chest out and drew my gut in slightly. Her purple lips curled into a sad smile, and something like a laugh coughed a bubble of blood in her throat. Her eyes sank and rose again, taking all of me in and then returning to my face.

"Do you want me to be honest?" She gurgled.

"That means I look fat to you."

Her eyes turned away from me again. Her blonde hair fell over them. A pin prick of rage pierced my neck. My teeth extended and a pool of saliva formed in my mouth. I stepped into the bathtub. Her white legs recoiled defensively exposing the upper part of her thigh. I could sense the delicate pulse of fresh blood in the artery. I looked at her face trying to make her it look exactly like the one who left me.

I tried to paint her eyes in my mind, shorten her nose, widen her mouth, and imagine. I imagined her. I imagined Heather. Thinking the name made me hungrier. I imagined her lying, bleeding, in the tub and not a prostitute with the same hair. I crouched low in the tub, a stream of her blood ran between her legs, soaked my knees and settled into a closed drain. I ran my teeth along the inside of her thigh; it jolted slightly as my mouth neared the artery. Pull back, you're not even that hungry. I looked up at her face once again, hoping that she would look more like Heather. Her eyes were fixed on something on the far wall. I hovered a tooth above the pulsing artery, ready to plunge in and lose myself for a few seconds of silence.

"Where's your girlfriend?" she asked, a matter-of-fact gurgle of blood in the back of her throat.

I broke into a cold guilty sweat. What did she know? How did she know that I had a girlfriend? I should just finish it and-

"Her toothbrush is still on your sink. Her razor, too. Unless you use Lady's Schick." I turned and saw what she was gazing at. The toothbrush and razor gazed back at me. As I tried to stammer an excuse, I could feel my gums close around my teeth, my mouth went dry and glass shattered inside of me. I wept miserably between the prostitute's legs. I felt a weak arm drape itself around my heaving shoulders. An unexpected and undeserved comfort. I took her pale arm and wrapped it around myself, a shield from everything. I noticed the ragged puncture marks on her wrist and the puncture on my hand. I wasn't hungry any more.

She was on my kitchen counter sipping orange juice made from a can of concentrate I found in the back of my freezer. Her blood stained dress was replaced with a t-shirt and sweats. She played with the heel of one of her pumps while she kicked her feet back and forth. She looked small perched on my counter, sipping juice. She looked human. I looked away and squeezed blood out of the dress into the sink. I couldn't bring myself to look her in the eyes. With her neck and wrists bandaged in gauze she was indistinguishable from the crumpled form in my bathtub.

"Does this mean I'm going to be like you?" she asked, spinning her high heel with the tip of her finger.

"I don't know. I'm new myself." I wrung the dress again and A torrent of blood and water poured into the drain.

"Did she turn you? Sorry, I only know the movie terms."

"Those are the only ones I know," I admitted.

"So, did she *turn* you?"

"Yeah."

"Do I look like her? Is that why you picked me?"

"Your hair. Her hair was like that."

"Oh."

I saw the blonde bob plop into the sink where I was idly playing with the folds of the dress. "Her hair was like that?"

I looked up. Her hair was chestnut brown under a wig cap, with a mess of bobby pins holding it in place. She pulled out the pins, and pulled the wig cap off, earth-dark hair tumbled to her shoulders.

"I guess I shouldn't have worn that wig, huh?" She managed a weak smile, her lips still blue around the edges. Guilt crucified me.

"Maybe, you should go,"

I turned to her. She had moved soundlessly behind me. She had the spike of the high heel pushed against my chest. My heart beat faster, seemingly trying to push the spike heel away with every pound. I couldn't remember the last time that I felt its motion stir within me but there it was, strong and terrified.

"Is this why you took my shoes off first?" I imagined the heel sinking into my chest.

I imagined it piercing my heart.

"Look at me."

I drew my eyes slowly past her lips. For a second I thought she was Heather. Strength had returned to her eyes and I could feel her pushing the heel through my shirt, deep into my chest. I wanted her to. I wanted her to pierce me and send me to nothingness. She dragged the tip of the heel across my chest.

"Would this kill you?"

"I think I'm dead."

"Does it hurt?"

"No more than being alive."

"I want it." She withdrew the heel from my chest, and let it hang coquettishly on her finger. There was a touch of cinder in her eyes and I knew that it was true. She laughed gaily. "I mean, if you want me to be like you. If you want- I don't know- a friend."

I thought of every day that I had stayed awake. I felt Heather's fingers slowly finding unconscious purchase within mine. I smelled the warm salt of life, and sex, and love in my empty apartment and I wanted her. I wanted her to be the answer to all of that. I licked my lips and felt my teeth unsheathing from my gums. I felt my chest. There was no heartbeat. Just a phantom muscle throbbing at nothing.

"I mean," she continued, "Don't you get lonely?" Before she was able to finish the word I fell upon her.

I dropped her blood-soaked dress to the floor, she dropped the shoe, the gauze from her wrists and neck followed. I sunk my hand into her dark hair. My body knew what to do even though my mind didn't.

A shriek issued from her mouth, I jerked her head back, silencing her. Iron and sugar, iron and sugar. I could smell it again. She began a dizzy collapse to the floor. I kept my teeth sunk deep into her neck, drunk, high, red pulsating and clouding the outlines of my vision. Iron and sugar. When we finally clattered together against the floor, I was licking the last bits of ruby from the punctures in her neck. She was still alive, because I could hear her laughing.

I didn't think about Heather.

It was 10 A.M. Finally, I slept.

I woke up before her. A crimson stain spread across my floor like black\red velvet. I cursed as I tried to remember if the security deposit to my apartment covered carpets. I leapt to my feet and tried to figure out what would take out bloodstains.

As I was daubing uselessly at the puddle, an ancient box of baking soda in my hand, a deep ragged breath pulled into her chest and she coughed up another flood of blood where I had been daubing. I sifted some more baking soda into the pool of blood and then gave up on the security deposit.

She sat up straight, blinking incredulously, as if trying to remember a drunken night. She looked down, noticing she was still wearing my clothes. I didn't move. I didn't breathe.

She sat blinking. She stretched an arm, twisted an ankle, and ran her tongue along her teeth, searching for what was different. She chuckled a bit. Took a deep breath. She looked at me. I slowly lowered the box of baking soda.

"That's really beautiful," she said, looking over my shoulder.

I turned, sitting in the puddle. Cutting through the blinds the moon had floated up, an unusually inky sky for a city. She strode across the room barefoot leaving bloody little footprints. I stood up, walked to the window. The blinds clattered up and the chord hissed as it caught. I felt her approach behind me. The best cure for loneliness is a stranger.

"Did it work?"

"I don't know, how do you feel? Hungry?"

"No. Not hungry." I was kind of hungry so I was hoping that she was as well.

"Do you want to go out there?"

She put a hand on the window, a foggy handprint hushing along the length of her pale fingers.

"I think I do."

"I LOVE THIS!!"

The sound of her voice echoing down the darkened alleyway somewhere between the Mann Chinese Theatre and Madame Tussaud's Wax Museum. She was kicking a bloody stump that was once a Japanese tourist. After two blocks of walking she became ravenous. I was shifting nervously from foot to foot, hoping that she would eat before anyone noticed. It was late, and no one was out on Hollywood Boulevard but a couple of trannys talking on the corner, and a homeless man in a wheelchair.

I coughed loudly, hoping that it would mask the sound of her crushing bones. I felt my phantom pulse return; blasting in my ears. I could hear her laughing, near hysteria, it almost sounded as if she were crying from joy between each annihilating blow. I was beginning to think that this was a mistake.

When I looked back at her she was holding the tourist by his or her (I couldn't tell at this point) camera strap, and slamming the body back into the ground. I was embarrassed. I never liked killing much. I just liked eating. It looked like she was the opposite.

"Have you. Um." I began.

"What!?" The sound of another shattering kick ricocheted down the alleyway. I shut my eyes against the sound.

"Have you, tried eating? Yet?"

"Oh. No. I just wanted to make sure he (it was a he) is good and dead!"

"He's dead! I think that he's dead. And if he isn't dead, usually they die, when you, you know, drink their blood... And stuff. Maybe you should just try and..."

"Yeah. Okay, what do I do?"

"I don't know. Just dive right in! Just go! Now! Because, it's getting late and stuff."

"Okayokay!

I sighed and wiped some sweat off my brow, only to be jolted again by the tourist's head being slammed on the dumpster. I thought about running away, but I felt responsible for her in some way.

A police cruiser passed.

I took out my cell phone and pretended to look for a signal.

"Okay, I'm done."

She was covered in blood, like a toddler gets covered in Spaghettios. She drew quick elated breaths.

"You know, while I was killing the eating the whatever- you know-

"What? What is it? And stay in the alley. Please, can you stay in the alley?

"Yeah, yeah. Just…"

"What?"

"What's your name?

My pulse stopped. I blinked twice.

"Andy. My name is Andy."

She giggled and began stropping the blood on the pants that I had lent her.

"What?" I demanded. Impatient and paranoid.

"No, nothing- That's just what I was calling myself. With an "I" at the end, but I was calling myself Andi. Small world. So. Andy. What do you want to do now?" She smiled broadly and wiped her lips with the back of my shirtsleeve.

She was a kid at a firing range. A junkie with a full sack. She was hungry in a city, and some small appetite began to cry for more. I fell in love with part of her. I was afraid of the rest.

I will do whatever you want to do. I will do anything. I am yours.

We took back streets and alleyways. The only people we saw were Hassidic Jews walking home quickly along darkened boulevards. We snuck back to my apartment, trailing bloody footprints. She washed. I found an old pair of jeans and a top that Heather had left. She emerged from the shower smelling like soap and asphalt. She leaned against the bathroom door still buzzing from her first kill. She wanted to go out again, the night was young and we had all day to sleep.

As we walked along the empting streets, the backs of our hands began to brush one another. Effortlessly our hands linked. I explored the crevasse made by the knuckle of her thumb, the warm flesh of her palm. I traced a thumb in slow unconscious circles around the back of her hand. For a minute, a feeling fluttered within me that I would call happiness.

The dollar movie theatres on the outskirts of Hollywood smelled like urine. She wanted to see that vampire movie that had moistened the crotches of adolescents everywhere. Irony had not escaped us though our heartbeats had. I had spent long days detesting the boy-band good looks of the alabaster skinned actor playing the lead vampire. But somehow, walking with her hand in mine, I would go anywhere. I would do anything. So long as her hand was in mine, I was as immortal as the night sky.

We sat in the darkened theatre. It was mostly empty save for a couple of ghostly forms occupying a scattering of seats. An old sleeping man who looked as if he had grown to be a part of the chair. Two giggling stoners were sneaking hits from a pipe of pungent smelling weed. A teary-eyed blonde who blew her nose behind us and took swigs off of a hidden bottle of wine. There was a small child leaning forward in the front row as if he could will the movie to click to life faster. An employee of the theatre walked slowly across the front of the house, a red wand dangling out of his hand. He stopped at center, silhouetted by the soundless beginnings of a preview. The projection showed upside down, and then righted itself.

"Enjoy the show." The employee spoke through a mechanical voice box that he applied to his throat. My mind kept leaping back to the image of Andi covered in blood and the glee with which she crushed the life out of the tourist.

"I snuck something in." She turned to me, smiling in the twilight of the previews. She removed a small bag of chocolates from her bag.

"It just felt wrong to come to the movies without any chocolate." She grabbed my jaw and gently opened it. She placed a chocolate on my tongue and ran her fingers along my top row of teeth. Her fingers tasted like blood still, the chocolate tasted like ash, but I smiled any way.

"Good?"

I nodded. The movie sprang to the screen. The hero did some heroic things. The heroine did some heroic things. Angels flew and vampires fought ghouls. We laughed effortlessly. Slowly, slowly our heads rested on one another. Our cheeks met. Our lips met. I tasted blood with a faint flicker of chocolate, and I was hungry.

When the movie let out we walked delirious and happy along the empty Hollywood streets. The houses were painted a milky blue from the over-full moon swelling above us. A slight breeze rustled the trees and a car passed on the unseen freeway. The streets belonged to us and with every lazy step we grew taller, my stomach sunk lower, my face was more perfect. As she stole a glance at me, I could tell that I had become beautiful in night.

"What part did you like the best?" she asked, clutching closer to my shoulder. The movie was terrible but so tinged with the rose of her touch that it was magnificent.

"Everything. I liked everything the best."

We returned to my apartment. The floor was covered in blood stains and there was with a pile of tacky pumps in the corner. The sun began to show it's first golden rays over the pacific ocean but we wouldn't see it. Sleeping in one another's arms we were deader than dead. We were grey smoke vapor, and the distant memory of something that may have never happened. We disappeared into each other.

Every night the sun would go down and I would wake to find her pacing at the window. Blinds drawn and watching for the moon to come up. She ached to get out onto the streets.

"I think we should go out now," she said, leaning on the doorway with a playful grin flickering across her face.

"It's too crowded," I replied, shoveling the pile of pumps into a trash bag.

"I know it's too crowded. I like that it's too crowded. I like that it's too crowded a lot." She approached me from behind but I didn't turn to look at her. She ran a hand up my spine, and the nape of my neck. She grabbed a handful of my hair and pulled my head back. "It means that you have to be careful. It means that you could get caught doing something bad. It means that you have to hunt."

I could smell iron on her breath.

And that was how she had me. Every night she would find something, or someone new. Some place public. Some place well-lit. Someone strong. Someone fast. Always something new. The police officer was the first.

She positioned me in the alley and brought my hand to her neck. My hand wrapped the whole way around her thin neck. She leveled her eyes at me and gave me a closed teeth grin. The pulse in her neck had stopped only a week or so ago, and she didn't seem to miss her heart.

"Just go with it. Have fun." She winked. Then she began screaming bloody murder. She held my hands to her and jerked from left to right. Tears rising in her eyes and mock horror exploding on her face. I squeezed a thumb into her throat and gripped harder. My heartbeat fluttered to life, as the police officer noticed us

When the officer approached she broke my grip and ran towards him, tears streaming down her face. As he clasped handcuffs on me she opened the back of his head with his own nightstick. She was magnificent. She sat on the cruiser kicking her feet with the key to the handcuffs dangling between her fingers.

"Did you have fun?" she asked as we hid in plain sight. We were just another couple walking along Hollywood Boulevard, looking at the stars in the pavement.

Then there was the stuntwoman. We took her while they were filming and feasted quietly under one of the trailers as the director looked at his script, trying to find out where the vampires came in.

We attacked who we wanted.

Then there was the Australian tour group. They were taking the night time "Haunted Hollywood" tour. As they walked from location to location, we snapped them up. First the stragglers on the edges of the group. Then the bigger ones, the stronger ones. They all thought that it was a part of the tour. They giggled and flirted, feigned being more afraid than they were as another of their group disappeared into a hallway in the Cecil Hotel. For awhile they were charmed. They were until the tour guide's head rolled down the hallway. They stared at it unblinking, with dumb smiles on their faces. They wanted the dark side of Los Angeles and we were it. They wondered, *'wait, is this real?'* Then, from around the corner, she came tearing after them. The remaining Aussies bolted down the hallway and went clattering down the stairs of the Cecil.

She paused outside where I was waiting, crouched by a dumpster.

"It's a chase!" she said, breathless.

I leapt to my feet and tore off after them.

We ran off in separate directions after separate Australians. Mine was tall, lean, and athletic looking, a mess of dirty blonde dreadlocks bounced as he ran. I was surprised that I was keeping up with him. I wasn't heaving for breath. My legs felt like they could go for days. As he mounted a fence and swung his feet over I jumped it easily. I could hear nothing but my phantom heartbeat and the pounding of our shoes in the alley. When I matched speed with him, I grabbed his shirt and threw him against a dumpster.

He was on his knees clutching his shoulder which was twisted at an impossible angle. His collarbone was broken and a couple of shattered teeth hung in his mouth. I stared at him. It had been so long since I had seen myself that I had no idea what I looked like. In my victim's eyes, I saw horror and I received no pleasure from it. He tried to stammer some syllables but all he could do was weep and with shaking hands open his wallet. He shook out American and Australian dollars and he finally got a word out his mouth trailing spit shards of teeth.

"Please."

I don't like killing I just like eating. But I wasn't hungry. I left him broken in the alley towards the glimmering street.

I told her that I killed him. I made up horrific details. I told her that he begged. She told me that she loved me.

We owned the city.

We could take anyone.

Even so-

Slowly, I stopped feeling the thumping in my chest.

I never ate any more. I chased. I helped her. I broke arms and smashed teeth. I did things that I never thought that I would. My chest felt hollow like a tin drum. I didn't eat any more so I lived off of her smile. I drank her laughter and for a moment a every night between the laughter and the screams I felt the beating of my phantom muscle. I pantomimed muggings and lost dogs. Alleys and parking lots became our theatres and where she was the director, I was the leading man. Finally the beating in my chest became faint illusion, like the memory of my face.

I pulled the woman into the alleyway by her hair. I just wanted her out of sight and I had no intention of killing her. I placed a hand on her mouth and we both listened to a series of wet cracks echoing down the adjacent alleyway. The pounding in my chest was long gone and I had not felt hungry in weeks. Sparing my victims was the only thing that made sense any more. I crouched low over the woman and her eyes met mine.

"Shhhh. If she knows that you're alive, she will kill you."

I didn't remember what I looked like, but in the eyes of this victim I was merciful. I hoped she wouldn't blow it. Then I walked out of the darkness wiping imaginary blood off of my mouth. She was kicking a pair of legs under a broken down Carolla. She stopped kicking and looked at me, silhouetted in the neon lights of Santa Monica Boulevard.

She eyed me up and down.

"You need to eat more. You're so skinny." She smiled her smile, but there was something behind it now. Disappointment. Maybe even disgust. She herself had already grown several sizes. Layers of muscle and fat had laid themselves over her child-like frame. She was unrecognizable from the skeleton in the blonde bob wig that I had almost killed in my bath tub.

She went back to kicking, trying to wedge the legs perfectly between the undercarriage of the car and the concrete of the alley. I approached, hoping that she would stop and we could leave.

"I've got it!" she forced a laugh. "I'm almost done, don't worry about it."

She gave the legs one more powerful kick. Blue and red lights played beneath the car. A child's stick-like legs went into tiny-sneakers with red and blue lights along the soles. Her gaze returned to me.

"It was quick," she said by way of an excuse.

She brushed past me, not wanting to see my expression. I stood, stunned, as I heard the clack clack clack of her shoes down the alleyway. We had an agreement. The lights on the shoes slowly died and the darkness beneath the undercarriage of the car swallowed the child's feet. Suddenly I wanted to be home again. I wanted to be watching T.V. and waiting for the sun to rise.

Her footsteps stopped. My victim had begun to weep softly. It echoed in the darkness. She stopped and saw my victim left where I had dragged her. A hand locked over her mouth, trying to keep in every last whimper.

She looked back at me, but I couldn't see her face.

We both had secrets now.

Every night she wanted more. She devoured. She came back caked in blood with asphalt scrapes and oil stains crisscrossing her legs. She looked like she had been chewed apart by the city, and she loved it. I would sit on the couch, looking for my infomercial while she showered. She would kiss me on the back of the head and with a warm liquid smile on her face and say:

"I had a wonderful night. Why didn't you come out?"

"Not hungry."

"You should eat something. Don't want to leave me alone, do you?"

"No." I said, blankly. No meaning. Just a sound.

She fell off to sleep in my arms and I waited for the infomercial. I wanted to see the host's shiny white teeth and his starched collar. I wanted to see the set made to look like an opulent suburban home. I wanted to see easy laughter and clear consciences. I wanted to see mountains of food being prepared easily in just seconds with just a touch of the blender. I wanted to see them taste, and smell. I wanted to feel the joy rising within them as they ate and were filled. I wanted to be one of them.

Her fingers were laced in mine and I could see specks of copper red that she wasn't able to shower off. I brushed away a couple strands of her hair and found the two neat puncture wounds in her neck.

The sun was beginning to climb in the sky and then I heard the laughter. I heard the stacking of crates and the setting up of tent poles. It must be Saturday. It had to be Saturday. The farmers market was being set up outside my window.

I untwined myself from her, setting her head down gently. She smiled and rolled over. I got the window stick and opened a peephole in my blinds. I watched people begin milling about. A couple with a squirming baby in a carriage were greeted by their fruit vendor and he popped some black berries into each of their mouths. The mother laughed as the father rolled the carriage back and forth while they talked.

And there he was. Drenched in sunlight and giving a demonstration in one of the tents. The host from the infomercial. I could hear his lilting English accent, but I couldn't make out what he was saying. I heard the high whine of the blender as he demonstrated its ability to make smoothies. He poured tall cool glasses of mango smoothies for the audience that had gathered around him. Hunger pierced my stomach and my throat was arid. My mouth poured with saliva and…

I…

wanted…

that. I wanted whatever he had. I wanted whatever they were eating. Nothing else could plug the black hole that had opened in my gut but what they had.

I tossed the window stick to the ground where it lay in a pool of sunlight. I turned to her sleeping form on the couch, and for a second she looked small again, innocent even. I let my fingertips brush along her neck and through her hair as I walked to the door. She loved this life; I just loved to eat.

I opened the door to my apartment complex. A long, green lawn doused in sunlight separated me and them. A razor's edge of pure white light cut inches in front of my feet. In the distance I heard the whine of the blender. I heard ice being crushed with overripe berries. I smelled wet concrete and freshly cut grass. I heard laughter.

I took a step, and the hunger went away.

L.A. History 4

The Abridged Corrected History of Los Angeles
"Heretics"
1911-1940

In 1911, the first film company opened in a small town called Hollywood. This was a newly incorporated portion of Los Angeles that was roughly divided into Central, North and West Hollywood. Black and white films were projected in smoke filled cinemas and nickelodeons entranced audiences across the world. As war raged across Europe, the original home of the cinema, Hollywood became ubiquitous with the movie industry. It also became synonymous with the god-like power of being known. Film Critic, B.F. Andaman, in her award-winning dissertation, The Crucible of Gods, explains in great detail why the allure of Hollywood is such an unusual feature in the history of Los Angeles.

"From its earliest days, Los Angeles has been in a tug-of-war. On one side, benevolent gods, prayers of the faithful, and the occasional unicorn. On the other side, blood sacrifice, demon worshipers, and the usual dragon. The city was as black and white as the projected images of Greta Garbo, and Charlie Chaplin. However, Hollywood changed everything. RKO, Paramount, Warner Brothers, and Columbia pictures gave the lowliest farm hand in rural America and the waitress at a country greasy-spoon one chance. If they took that chance they could become Gods or Demons themselves. They could join the pantheon of the worshiped

along with Atlas, Joan of Arc, and Buster Keaton. Luck, money, talent, determination, and sex appeal remain the stations of the Hollywood cross. Those who take up the cross understand that they will hang themselves upon it to be remembered forever or they will be stripped naked, flayed and left for dead for absolutely no reason. It is a marvelous and terrifying business. It is a place like no other"

More and more people poured in to the borders of the once Spanish Pueblo. People came seeking new lives in the desert by the sea, those with pretty faces and empty heads, those with their pasts set ablaze, those who prayed to dark gods, and those with pure souls that were empty as drums. They all had only one thing in common. They were thirsty. They came to the desert to quench their thirst.

Water, water

One could almost hear God and Satan slapping one another on the back as they enjoyed good belly laughs while the people of Los Angeles jumped from foot to foot. They bestowed fires, earthquakes, floods, and droughts. Still, people came in droves. In an effort to channel some of the run off of the flood plain and put a thumb in the eye of God himself, the Army Corps of Engineers decided to bury the river in concrete, slowing the water to a trickle of sewage and industrial detritus. This, and the growing worship of celebrity, angered God greatly while amusing Satan dearly. God drank the water from the sand and left the hundreds of thousands of Angelinos nothing but the Pacific Ocean full of salt water to stare blankly at, hoping for a drink. Even Satan thought that this move was a bit much. He decided to go into the film business.

God and William Mulholland

There are few times in history when a mortal man does such furious battle with God that he is respected as a worthy adversary. History will always remember William Mulholland and his Los Angeles Water Department as the man who spat in the face of God himself. On an unrelated note, he was Irish.

Mulholland's formative years were spent terrorizing religious schools in his native Belfast. When he was seven his mother died, causing him to renounce his belief in God. He was routinely beaten by his father and visited by demons seeking to make deals with him for his eternal soul.

He turned his back on all of them and left for The Royal Navy. The ocean made sense to him, ropes and pulleys made sense to him. Foundations of stone, the moldable earth, and the laws of physics were his holy trinity. He was cheap and quick to anger. He was near mad with self-satisfaction and he had a vision of changing the world forever. He was the perfect Angelino. He was a man who looked into the desert and saw the oasis that he could carve out of it.

He was given a job digging ditches in San Pedro. He was the only ditch digger to survive, as the rest were consumed by The Great and Terrible Sea Monster. A recent exhibition in the Fowler Art Gallery shows a lithograph of William Mulholland and The Great and

Terrible Sea Monster enjoying a bottle of Irish Whiskey and playing Spades. The Freemasons feared Mr. Mulholland as he was neither motivated by money or glory, they could not very well kill him, so they decided to use him.

The Los Angeles City Council hired Mulholland for his superior engineering skills and distaste for a belief in a divine creator. He set about solving Los Angeles's water problem through an intense regiment of mathematics, soil sampling, and drunken bare-knuckle Irish boxing.

On one of his many prospecting missions, Mulholland tasted the rancid, demon filled water of the Los Angeles River. He spat it on the ground, stripped naked, and railed at the sky. God unleashed a torrential flood on the Irishman and attempted to wash him out to sea. He was saved by his once drinking buddy, The Great and Terrible Sea Monster. As he stood, naked, shivering, and half drown on the beach of San Pedro, he conceived of one of the greatest engineering projects of the twentieth century. If God gave him a desert, he would make it an oasis through stone, mortar, and ferocious determination.

Between 1908 and 1913 with the help of thousands of laborers William Mulholland created one of the most complex systems of aqueducts and reservoirs that the industrial world had ever seen. If the water of the Los Angeles River was poisoned by the creator himself, Mulholland would go elsewhere. He went to Owens Valley and he found clear sources of fresh water. If there was no pure water in Los Angeles he would expand the reach of Los Angeles until he drank up all the water in California. He made his case to the Los

Angeles City Council, who in turn made their case to the Freemasons, who in turn made their case to The Golden Owl, who blessed them with visions of horrifying glory. They approved the creation of the Los Angeles Water Department.

The residents of Los Angeles staggered the dusty streets thirsty for the 8 years Mulholland spent in construction. When the day finally came for the water to begin flowing on a hot day in November 1913 all eyes were on the Irish transplant. Mulholland stood atop the newly constructed dam, his eyes shadowed by an understated fedora. The turnout was enormous. Mulholland looked into the crowd and saw them all for what they were. They were the sons and daughters of conquerors, sorcerers, demons and angels. They were as different as the stars in the sky and those being carved on Hollywood Boulevard. But they all held two things in common: this city and their thirst. They were all thirsty.

Mulholland was slated to make a speech that day. He did it in five words, "There it is, take it." With that he flipped the switch and water came pouring from hundreds of miles away into the Los Angeles River Basin. A roar went up from the citizens of Los Angeles, and even the Freemasons gave the engineer polite golf-claps. Mulholland later wrote about the day in his journal.

"I walked off the dais, and I heard the water flowing. I thought of my mum lying dead in her bedclothes. I thought of the war I waged on the man upstairs since that day. I put my hands together and I prayed. I prayed clear and true, and I know that he heard what I said. 'I win.' I felt a tremble in the ground and I dared him to do his worst. The aqueduct is perfect"

Spilled Water

On March 12th 1928 the St. Francis Dam failed catastrophically. Over 600 people died, making it one of the largest civil engineering disasters in American history. When asked for a comment, Mulholland said, "I only envy the dead, for they feel no guilt."

Something was broken in Mulholland after the collapse of the dam, though he was not frightened into submission for long. Eventually he was tapped by President Roosevelt to help with the Panama Canal. He agreed because, quote, "I wanted to bore a hole on a continent."

God and William Mulholland kept a respectful distance after that.

Wolf Skin

You came out here to be a killer like everyone else. But you weren't like everyone else. You had the inside track. You had a way around things. People said things to you that made you realize that you could kill anything you put your mind to. Those people are in the town that you came from. You don't know when or if you will return to the town you came from but you don't care.

When you left your racist, but-funny-when-she's-racist Aunt Gloria said that Los Angeles was full of homos. She has always used the word homos to mean both sexes and some minorities. She warned you against becoming a homo yourself, and suggested that you find a church. A real church, not a "latte and bare midriff" church. You laughed, because you knew this was her way of showing that she cared about you. You promised her that you would not become a homo. She hugged you a little harder at the airport when you left. Now you are here, and she is there. You are in your car and she is probably in church.

You're driving towards the dense knot of freeways downtown, where the 110, 101, and the 10 collide into one another like waves of asphalt. You want to get home to West Hollywood. You live in West Hollywood because that's where the action is. You followed the action along with everyone else. They don't know that you're a killer. You turn rap music up in your car and step on the gas.

You come upon a wall of red brake lights. They approach you faster than you can react because you are busy accepting awards in your mind. You are making a speech underscored by rappers calling people bitches blaring out of your speakers. You associate with the rappers not the bitches. You slam on the brakes as hard as you can. The car slides. It shouldn't slide. There is no reason that it should be sliding. Your car slides into the Lexus in front of you and dents the bumper. Your face flushes. The fantasy crumbles around you. You want to run back to your small Midwestern town. You want to get a job as a faceless school teacher. You want to marry someone pale and kind. You want to grow fat and forget that you ever had dreams of being a killer in a big city. You dented a Lexus. Your life is over.

Everyone is stopped around you. You can barely make out the guy next to you because frost has developed on the inside of your window. You open the door and try to step out. Your seatbelt grabs you. You wrestle yourself out of the seatbelt and step onto the pavement.

You slip. Your legs go out from under you before you even realize it. You are on your back. You are staring up at a steel grey sky. You have never seen a sky like this in Los Angeles. You don't look up at the sky that often but this one looks different.

A snowflake lands on your nose. You sit up. A chill runs through you. You are sitting in a thin layer of snow on the freeway tarmac. You stand up to find everyone around you standing up and looking at the sky. Some of them open their mouths to catch snowflakes. The woman standing next to the Lexus looks like a woman who would stand next to a Lexus. She stares blankly up at the sky. She is not shocked or dismayed. She is not impressed or underwhelmed. She wears a red blazer and dangerous high heels. She scowls at the sky like it will stop snowing because of her displeasure. She doesn't notice the dent in her car. She has more pressing concerns now. Namely, why the hell is it snowing?

More cars come sliding into the mass of snow-covered automobiles. The sounds of cars colliding, metal twisting, and the occasional screaming dies down. The only sound you can hear is the delicate impact of snowflakes touching down on the cooling metal of the totaled cars. The LAPD places barricades along the freeway. People staring up at the sky become irate and demand answers of the equally confused police officers. Nobody has any answers. In the distance, a news helicopter is forced into a quick descent. An explosion follows, rumbling over East L.A.

The LAPD officers breathe warm breath into their hands. Everyone waits to be told what to do. No signals come through from anyone with authority. Cellphones are consulted and consulted again. Nothing. They are frozen blocks. Phantom rings and text messages send people clutching at their pockets for some kind of signal. You begin to feel very alone. You can see the sun sinking low over the mountain of twisted metal that has become the 110 freeway. You are starting to get cold and it is starting to get dark.

The people on the freeway get into their cars and run the heaters. Warm and alone, they search glove compartments for stale pretzels and linty Sour Patch Kids. You jab at your radio dial looking for contact with someone outside of the freeway. You would take a persons life to listen to NPR. Sadly, such an option is not currently being offered. You think about putting on one of your rap CDs. Because your car is old, and you are older than people think, you have a large plastic wallet of rap CDs beneath your driver's side seat. You decide silence is a better option than false bravado.

You see people approaching. A group of nomads walk between the cars looking for one that will let them in. The heater has gone out in their cars and they're looking to warm up a bit before night falls completely over the freeway. The woman in the Lexus takes one look at the group and waves them on without unrolling her window. They come to your window. You're afraid that the conversation will be really awkward. You're afraid that they are killers and rapists. You do not want to be raped and killed. You wonder what Jesus would do and then you think of your Aunt Gloria. What would Aunt Gloria do?

One of the people knocks on your window. The leader of the group is a middle-aged man who looks older. His face has lines carved by a special type of hard living. His jaw hangs half open puffing icy breath after icy breath. His hair is thin and stringy. He wears two children's sweatshirts tied around him like a cape. They barely cover his hairy arms. He grins trying to look good-natured but the ragged holes in his teeth have the opposite effect. He has a Mexican woman and a teenage girl with him. Your heater is beginning to cough and sputter and you wonder how much longer it will last. You see snow collecting on the shoulders of the people outside your car. You wonder how long it will last.

You wave the nomads on. This is your heat. This is your car. You bought a car with a working heater and when it snows you are going to be warm. You did not come out here to care about other people. Charity and kindness are fairy tales for chumps, and that guy was absolutely a murderer. You came out here to be the woman in the Lexus. Your windshield is badly fogged but you can see the taillights of the Lexus. You wonder if the woman is warmer than you are.

Your heater sputters to a stop. You hope that your body heat will keep the car warm through the night. You wish that you had let those people in. A deep onyx pit of guilt forms in your stomach. You promise Jesus that if you get out of this alive you will always give change to the homeless. You think back to the sad eyes of the Mexican girl those people may have turned into good friends after all of this was over. They may have been producers or famous DJ's. They may have kept you from shivering. You decide that you were wrong earlier. You open the door to call the nomads back.

A hot breath of warm air escapes like steam from inside of your car. You wish for a minute that you could grab some of the heat and shove it into the pockets of your thin sweatshirt. You can see the teenage Mexican girl passing between the snow covered cars behind you. She looks back. You smile broadly at her. Your smile is a homing beacon to warmth and companionship. Her caramel colored skin looks pale white in the failing light. She has refugee eyes. She is looking for home anywhere. She takes a step back towards your car.

The man and woman burst through the crack in the cars. They push past the girl and knock her into the snow. The man runs screaming past the woman who has lost her footing in the snow.

You turn back to see the source of their fear. An enormous wolf bounds from the darkness over a disabled Audi. It leaps onto the teenage girl. It's jaws wrap around her neck and mute her last scream with a quick wet SNAP. The cold still air lets you hear everything. Two more wolves leap onto the roofs of cars. The roofs crumple like soda cans. Their dagger-long claws sink through the metal of the cars. They howl. Their howls make your ribs vibrate with fear. You piss your pants and fling the door shut. You huddle into a ball, feeling the heat from your piss bleed out into the air.

Small clouds of breath puff from your chattering teeth. You want to wake up. You want to go home. Nothing that you wanted before matters now. You are sitting in your own cold urine. You hear heavy paws falling on metal outside. Everything is too loud. Every breath and heart beat sounds like an air horn. You move slowly. You have never moved so slowly. You peel the covers off your seat and the driver's side seat. You cover yourself as best as possible in the thin faux-sheep skin. You shiver. You silence your clattering teeth because you can still hear stalking paws in the snow. Or is that your heartbeat?

Your fingers have gone white. You tuck them into your armpits, and then between your legs, searching for any pocket of warmth. You wait for your car to fill up with your body heat. You wonder what the Mexican girl's name was. You begin to whisper with her like she is in the back seat. You ask her how old she is. You ask her what she wants to be when she grows up. You ask her if she is from Los Angeles. You explain that you are new here. You have big plans. You have big dreams.

Your windows are too fogged to see through. Your hands are too cold to feel. Outside you can hear the heavy footfall of wolves stalking between the cars.

You wake up with a start. You have no idea where you are. Your car. Cold. Did you get drunk last night and sleep in your car? You would do something like that, wouldn't you? Do you have work today? Why are your seat covers... no... no... That can't be.

A thin sheen of ice covers the insides of your windows. You try the ignition. It fights. It wheezes. It dies. You are cold. You are hungry. Before you drifted off to sleep last night, you found a pack of Rolaids in your glove compartment. You fell asleep with them rolled up in your hand. The Rolaids and the cold coffee in your cup holder are the only things that you have to eat. This makes you colder and hungrier. You can see bits of sunlight reflecting through the ice on the inside of your window. You wonder if the sun is beginning to melt away the ice. You wonder if people are coming to help.

You remember that you have a cellphone. You think that you're an idiot for not thinking about it before. You can't believe that you didn't pull it out. It's been your everything for as long as you can remember. Your friend, confidant, and secret lover was not there for you when you saw the girl get eaten. You remember her being silenced by the jaws of the wolf. You turn to the back seat and say good morning to her in Spanish. You accidently say "good afternoon" to her in Spanish but you don't know that.

You take out your cell phone. It remains a frozen block. You poke uselessly at the apps on the screen. You nudge it again and again assuming that you can wake it from its slumber. You compose a status update in your brain.

I would rather be eaten by wolves than be stuck in this traffic.

The thought makes you start to cry a little, but you're too hungry and too cold to let yourself cry. You put a hand to the icy window. The warmth from your hand melts the ice on the window just enough to see out of it. Through your handprint you can see some yellow sun playing off of a snow dune across from you.

Maybe this is it. Maybe it's all over. Maybe you can write a book about this. Maybe a web series. Maybe a podcast. It will depend on funding. Maybe you can talk to the woman in the Lexus. After all, she IS a woman in a Lexus. You need to leave your car.

You psych yourself up by remembering as much of the rap song that you were listening to last night. You pull the handle and push the door.

Nothing.

You push at it again. You can hear some ice splintering. You realize that you are frozen into the car. The ice was melted by the sun and then refrozen. You hold the handle open and kick at the door until it breaks free and swings wide open. You are not prepared for what you see.

You are surrounded by a forest of frozen skyscrapers. The freeway is choked with snowy cars and bloody tracks. Between them are weaving paths where people were chased down and consumed by wolves.

There are no carcasses except for a dead wolf that lies steaming near the snow-covered Lexus.

The woman stands over the dead wolf. She pulls at its skin and cuts the slippery red meat away from the fur with what appears to be her house key. Her mouth is clenched into a half frown as she digs deeper into the entrails. She still wears a red Prada blazer and a matching pencil skirt that she has hiked up to her thighs. She is kneeling in the snow. The effort from skinning the wolf is making steam float up from her body.

You realize that the wolf is bigger than any wolf you've ever seen in movies. You have never seen a wolf in real life. It's at least eight feet long. Cut down the center and splayed open it looks like a children's pool full of red ink.

"Are you okay?!" You hear yourself call out to her. Immediately you are embarrassed at the weakness in your voice. She jabs her house key into the guts of the wolf. Her wrist is dyed fire truck red up to the elbow. It matches her blazer. The the color of the Lexus matches the wolf carcass.

"You should get back in your car," she says through clenched teeth. She does not look up from her work.

"No! I mean... What is happening? Why is all of this *occurring!?* Who!?" You are not making sense, and you know that you are not making sense. The fear that you hear in your voice stokes the fear in your belly. The woman in the Lexus jabs her keys into the guts of the wolf. She stands up and pulls at its pelt.

"I don't understand a word you're saying. You should get back in your car before they come out again." She gives the fur a hard yank and entrails go tumbling out of it into the snow. She wraps the gore soaked fur around herself. She looks like The Red Queen from Alice In Wonderland. You can't tell if you think she is beautiful or terrifying.

"I don't have any food," you say, blank and honest. You feel small and cold. You can hear the approach of paws in the snow. You don't know how long you have to talk. She reaches in her car and pulls out a stack of Powerbars. She throws them into the snow. You scramble for the Powerbars. You clutch them to yourself like you can consume them by osmosis.

"Thankyouthankyouthankyou," you mumble. The woman in the Lexus lets her pelt fall open. She is holding a large silver revolver.

"Understand. That was not charity. It was a down payment. I need you to find bullets for me. You know where I am when you find them." Then she wraps the wolf skin around herself and steps into her car. There is nothing left of her but a pile of guts and a wolf's head.

You realize that you are alone. You are alone in the snow. The frosted windows of the cars stare at you unblinking. You know you are being watched. You turn and run back to your car, fling the door open. You look over your shoulder and you can see dark shoulders prowling lazily down the lane of cars. A wolf. You lock eyes with it.

Its eyes are without sense and mercy. All it knows is hunger, and the joy of hunger being sated. It launches off of its back haunches and bounds towards you. It is a big rig truck of hair, muscle, teeth, and claws. For a second you consider letting it take you. Adrenaline juices your system. You fling yourself into your driver's seat, put the seat back, and camouflage yourself with the faux-sheep skin covers.

You hear the wolf's claws catch in the ice and asphalt as it comes to a stop next to your door. You see the ice against the window darken in the shape of a mouth. It's a cruel shadow puppet. It lets out a *yip yip*. For a second you think it is cute, then it butts the side of your car with its head. You feel the side door crumple inwards toward you.

Bang!

The car rocks back and forth. You are searching frantically for something to protect yourself with. You search under each of the seats coming up with nothing but sticky pennies and lint.

Bang Bang!

The metal is beginning to give. You grab onto something hard and heavy. It's a heavy metal steering wheel lock. *The Club*. Your Aunt bought it for you before you left because she said the homos in Los Angeles steal cars. You clutch it to you and imagine the wolf's head bursting through the window. You imagine shattering its teeth and destroying its face.

Nails against your door. *It huffed and puffed. It huffed and puffed. It huffed and puffed,* is all you can think. You realize that you are screaming. Your screaming sounds like an animal. You see the wolf snap off your side mirror and chew it like a milk bone. You have The Club ready. You are ready. You are ready to die now.

The wolf lets out a craggy cough. It wheezes and you hear something spill into the snow. It snaps its teeth together once more and then collapses into the snow.

You wait. Steam is coming off of your sweaty palms. Your eyes are wide open, they are are glued to the ceiling of your car. There are cigarette burns on the ceiling of your car. You do not smoke. You have no idea how they got there. You hear yourself laughing. You look to the back seat and you imagine the Mexican girl. You reach back to grab her hand comfortingly, but she's not there. You know that she is not there but you do it any way.

Hunger was blanched from your system but you know that you have to eat. You tear open one of the Powerbars and bite into it. It's a waxy chemical vanilla. It's delicious. You want a million of them. If you get out of this you will eat nothing but Powerbars for the rest of your life. You save the last bite of the Powerbar. You shove it between the cushions in the backseat for the Mexican girl. She can eat it when she wants it.

You knock The Club against the window to see if the wolf responds. Nothing. You sneak your head up to the window. You wipe away some of the ice and look down.

The wolf is still as stone. You slip a hand in the door handle and push against it's huge hairy form. It's a heavy sack of muscle and flesh. It doesn't move. You push your way out into the snow with The Club prepped and ready.

You step out into the snow. The sun is already going down. How long have you been awake? How many days has it been? Never mind. Nothing matters except making sure the wolf is dead.

Its mouth is open and gaping. Shards of the side view mirror jut through its neck and glittering pieces of glass sparkle on its tongue. It's dumb and hungry. It's just dumb and hungry. You raise The Club over your head.

With every shattering blow you think, *thank you Aunt Gloria, thank you. I told you I would be fine out here.*

It is late. You think. You try to will yourself to sleep but you can't. You're too hungry. You hear howling. It comes up out of everywhere, the strings and bass of Satan's orchestra warming up. You hear paws marauding outside the car. You hope that they see the body of the wolf at your door and learn something from it. You hear more howling.

You hear an engine start up and rev. Howling stops. You wipe the ice off of the inside of your windshield. You see the tail lights of the Lexus spilling blood red light over the snow. You can hear Journey's *Don't Stop Believing* playing inside of the car at full volume. You can feel the cold eating into your bones. You know that if it gets in it will kill you. You look back at the Mexican girl. She looks sad.

You see a black wolf approaching the window of the Lexus. The window rolls down. The wolf bares its teeth and pulls back onto its legs, spring loaded. A manicured hand comes from the open window with a revolver. It delicately squeezes the trigger and the wolf's head disappears into a red mist. The hand goes back where it came from. The window rolls up. The music gets turned up.

You just fell in love with her in a way. She is a killer. You will find whatever she needs.

Hold on to the feelin
Streetlight People
Livin just to find emotion…

You fall asleep, knowing that tomorrow you will hunt.

You wrap your faux-sheepskin seat covers around yourself. The cold is beginning to eat you. Your pinkie fingers are red like raw hamburger left out since yesterday. Now you can't feel them so well. You wish that you had taken a first aid course, but when would you need to use it? You laugh to yourself. You eat a half of a Powerbar and leave the rest for the Mexican girl. You hope that she will warm up the car while you're gone.

The Lexus lies sleeping, in front of it is a welcome mat of hair and gore. You will get inside of that car. You close your car door and twist your hands around The Club. You want to feel bone yield under it again. The fear in your chest takes an easy right turn and becomes pure delicious rage.

The snow has frozen into jagged crags over the night. The blood, and hair, and asphalt mix together into a dense sludge beneath the frozen tundra. Every time your foot goes through you shudder from disgust and cold.

You remember walking through the snow-lined streets in your Midwestern town. You remember the joy of returning tired and cold to something wonderful boiling on the stove. Why did you think so much about catastrophe then? You thought you would be more of a hero than you are. You come to the first car that you're going to break into. You hope there is something good in it. The sun is sailing towards its apex, that is the warmest it will be all day and it is still below freezing. You can't afford another night in the cold.

You wipe ice and snow off the window of the Toyota Echo. You peek inside. No one. Nothing. Maybe the owner is breaking into your car right now. You think about all of the times that you wanted to smash glass and take things that didn't belong to you. A smile finds it's way to your face. You swing The Club.

The window caves in, throwing glass shards into the back seat glittering like rhinestones. You dive into the car. It's colder inside than it is outside. You rummage through the backseat, and the glove box. You come up with a vial of medical marijuana and a couple of skateboards; empty bottles of 5-Hour Energy and fast food containers. You do not know this person but you do not like this person. You feel no guilt at taking some rolling papers, and a vial of pot. No bullets. Your Aunt Gloria told you that everyone has guns in Los Angeles. Everyone has guns because of the gangs and the homos. Turns out that not everyone has guns.

You find a multi-tool with a knife and a saw in the back pocket of the driver's side seat. It looks like gold to you. You open and close the blade again and again. You want to feel it pushing into warm flesh.

You move to leave the car through the broken window. A wall of flesh and fur passes inches from your face. You can smell its fur, like wet earth and copper. You arrest your breath and exhale in a thin stream of steam. It continues down the line of cars, stopping to sniff the ground or urinate on a tire. It's just an animal. It's just a hungry dumb animal. You're a hungry smart animal. With a knife. You wait for it to turn a corner and then you creep out of the window

You hold The Club and the knife firm in your hands.

You have more hunting and stealing to do.

You move quietly from car, to car checking to see if the coast is clear before collapsing windows with The Club and diving in. Each of the cars is a life in a frozen moment. You rifle through high heels and gym bags. You find a Zippo lighter and a stack of headshots. Her name was Phyllis and you can burn her pictures to keep yourself warm. You stuff them in a gym bag along with resumes, demo CDs, and self-help books that want you to live your best life NOW. Everything will burn.

You back out of a car and find the man with the stringy hair and the crumbling teeth is in the snow with a rubber tube and a gasoline can. He wipes his mouth with the back of his arm. He is covered head to toe in sweatshirts, towels, and bed sheets. He looks like a pile of laundry with a gasoline can. You are aware of the multi-tool in your hand. You are aware of your club. He looks at the multi-tool with its knife out. He looks at The Club. Your hand twists around it tighter. Your fingers are beginning to go numb. If someone wants your club they will have to take your arm.

Snow begins to sprinkle down from the leaden sky. It collects in his eyelashes and in the hollow of your neck. It melts there and finds a way down to the small of your back. A tire iron slips out from one of his sleeves. This is not a threat, it is a statement of fact. His face does not change. He is bigger than you. You have often found yourself fantasizing about your ability to inflict violence on someone. You don't know if you could do it. You picture him somewhere else, a bank manager in a suit and tie, a stay at home dad making shells and cheese for his kids, a police officer writing up speeding tickets. You realize that you are holding your breath

A breeze blows. Earth and iron. Saliva. You both smell it. You have learned a lot in two days. Three? A week? You hear bending metal. You hear the approach of paws an appetite wants to be satisfied. Screaming metal. Breaking ice. There could be two, there could be three. They could already be surrounding you. Did you ever learn anything about wolves in school? Do you know anything about how they hunt? Was that a wolf?

A dark shape materializes from out of the snow behind the man with the stringy hair. It dwarfs the man. Its mouth hangs open and its golden eyes scan the him lovingly as if about to cuddle into him. He stands perfectly still. The wolf is glorious in size: eight, maybe nine feet tall. The wolf sniffs the man. The man stands still. His eyes closed. His tire iron trembles.

He throws his entire body behind the weight of the tire iron and swings it into the wolf's face. The sound of a baseball bat against a wet log. The wolf recoils and adjusts its jaw. You can hear the joint resetting itself as it yawns. The man makes a break for it.

Snap.

Before his foot lands, he is hanging limp in the mouth of the wolf: his neck between teeth, his left leg twitching until it quiets completely. The wolf places the man on the snow gently and paws at him. Nothing happens inside of you while you watch the man being devoured. Nothing. You wonder where you can find bullets. You wonder if the wolf has seen you. You turn around slowly. You catalogue where the body is so that you can return for the gasoline. The woman in the Lexus would be pleased if you got gasoline. You can never have enough to burn.

You turn around to find two wolves standing atop cars on either side of you. You were being hunted. Part of you knew that you were being hunted. At the end of the long line of frosted cars you see a bumper sticker, *Guns don't kill people. People kill people.*

It's not like a dream where no matter how hard you try you can't go any faster. Your biology moves for you. Your brain is in Sunday school in your small Midwestern town. You are talking with the little Asian boy whose parents died in a car wreck. Your shoe gains purchase on the ice. Your teacher tells him that God is testing him. You are leaping more than running, your body feels tight and loaded, like a red hot spring. You see the muscles in the wolves shoulders tighten and release as they leap. The Asian boy sits wide-eyed, he says that he wants to get a good grade on the test. The teacher says that if he loves Jesus he will. You are not faster than the wolves. They run along side you in milliseconds, in breaths.

Yip! Yip!

You feel their animal wheeze on the side of your face and it turns your stomach. A couple feet more. A couple feet more.

You dig your heels into the snow and arrest your speed. The wolves go flying past you. They leap onto their hunches and bear down, thin streams of hot drool pouring between their clenched teeth. The Sunday school teacher, pats him on the head and tells him that he is getting a good grade on the test. You let The Club fly out of your hand.

You see the glass caving inward. You feel hot breath that is almost sweet with rot. The jagged glass on the sides of the windows drag deep into your arms and sides as you go tumbling through the window into the back seat. Two heads burst through the smashed window, snapping and belching clouds of hot breath into the freezing interior. The metal on the side of the window bulges as the wolves vie for position. Their eyes are idiotic and hungry, but you, you are alive.

You can tell that you are alive because you're bleeding out of the deep trenches that have been dug in your arms. But you do not care. You are alive. You are so ultimately alive.

Snap snap snap.

"Ahhhh!!!!"

You scream at them. You scream at them because they're everything. They are your racist Aunt Gloria. They are the frost bite on your pinkies. They are the dead Mexican girl in the back of your car that you could have saved.

Snap snap snap.

"No! No! You will not! I'm not going to let you! Stop!"

You are outside of yourself looking in. You are screaming nonsense at the wolves as if they understand, as if you can reason with them. You flick out the blade of your knife.

Snap sn-

When the blade goes in it does not feel good. You feel the tip navigate through meat and gristle and bone. It reminds you that the wolf is meat and so are you. Its eyes roll. Your stomach lurches. You dry heave and threaten to spill the meager contents of your stomach. The wolf releases an agonized gurgle and slumps onto the ground, its massive head still perched on the window. The other wolf withdraws. It licks the neck of the wolf that you've impaled on your knife. It nudges the wolf. It does not respond. The living wolf looks at you and you think for a moment that you catch a bit of sadness in its eyes.

You want to explain that you're just hungry and cold and scared. The wolf nudges the corpse once more and then turns to leave. You can see that the sun is starting to go down. You pull the blade from the wolf's jaw and clean it on the seat cushions of the car. You put a hand on its face. The fur is smoother than you imagined. You put your cheek up against the wolf's and you feel its warmth beginning to drain out into the freezing air. You want to wrap yourself in its warmth. You think about your childhood dog. You think about lying on its stomach and listening to it breathe. Maybe you're there now. Maybe this is a vivid daydream from your childhood and you are about to wake up in your bed.

You open your eyes.

You laugh when you pop open the glove box and find a fresh box of ammunition. The sun is half gone behind the hazy clouds. You cannot make it back to your car by nightfall. The window is broken. You cannot keep the cold out. You roll a joint and smoke it while you think about this problem.

The weed hits you immediately. You sit in the back seat of the car looking at the dead wolf. You laugh a little bit at nothing in particular. You think about the woman in the Lexus. You think about her forearms bathed in blood. Great minds. Great minds. You open the knife again. You are going to survive.

When the morning comes, you are wrapped in a blanket of thick fur. The smell of the wolf has saturated every part of you now. It is no longer offensive to you. The feeling is beginning to come back into your pinkies and you can see the sun beginning to crest the horizon. You wonder if it is maybe a couple of degrees warmer. You wonder if the thaw is coming. You wonder what you will do if this all ends. You pocket the box of ammo. You grab The Club and your knife. You push what remains of the wolf out of the way as you step out of the car.

This icy air does not penetrate the fur. You remember the man from the night before. He had gasoline with him when you last saw him. You look down the line of frozen cars. He is laying in the same position that the wolf left him, only he is naked. The gas can is nowhere to be seen. The wolves must have been spooked off by something. Were there others? Were there scavengers? You plan to ask the woman in the Lexus.

You double back the way you came the night before. You realize that you are tracking yourself through the faint imprints your shoes left yesterday. How long have you been able to do this? Has it been a week? Two weeks? When was the last time that you ate? You think about the Powerbar in your car. Your stomach rouses. You would kill for a vanilla Powerbar, you think, then you realize, you *would* kill for a vanilla Powerbar. You would take a life for a vanilla Powerbar. How long has it been?

You pull your pelt tighter around yourself and you truck through the snow. You see a furry ear traveling along side a mini-cooper with a destroyed front end.

You drop to the ground next to a big rig and squeeze yourself into the shadows. The ear appears from behind the car. You ready your knife. You ready your club. You ready yourself to die. The ears are worn by a pink-faced middle-aged woman. A robe of wolf's fur wraps around her thick matronly shoulders. She carries a golf club, and a large bag of Cheetos. She crouches low to the ground and sniffs the air. She has survived this long. She must have learned quickly. You flick the blade back into your multi-tool. You wait for her to pass. Even in the frozen air you can smell the chemical cheddar cheese in the bag. Your tongue and stomach spasm. She has skinned a wolf, she should be left alone. You step out from under the big rig, and make sure to step when she steps so that she does not hear you in the snow.

Your car lies covered in a partial pyramid of snow. You reflexively check over both of your shoulders. There is no sound. You recognize your car because it is still wedged in the back of the Lexus, its front fender bent at a rakish angle towards the ground. You laugh a plume of breath into the frozen air. That would have been a months rent. What is rent again? Rent is a box of bullets and a warm place to sleep. Rent is a wolf's skin and the ability to take one.

You open your car door and sit in the drivers seat. You look in the backseat. There is no one there. You remember that you shoved a piece of Powerbar in the cushions of the back seat. You retrieve it and put it in your mouth. It has almost frozen solid, and it doesn't taste as good as you remember. It is something though. It is something to fill you. That is what matters- that you are filled.

You feel the weight of the box of bullets in your pocket. It's time to go home. This car has nothing for you any more. You remember buying it from friends of your parents outside of the church. They gave it to you at a bargain because they wanted to support your dreams. They wanted to let you know that you could always come back home. You wonder if they have been eaten by wolves. You wonder if this winter is everywhere or just on this stretch of freeway. You realize that it doesn't matter, because you are on this stretch of freeway. This is your stretch of freeway.

You step out of your car. The frozen skyscrapers gaze down at you like steel titans. The cars are a frozen graveyard. Snow begins to fall again. The sun begins to set again. This time it is a bright brilliant pyre behind a falling sheet of ice. You pull a hood of fur over your head.

You can see your face in the frozen glass. Your eyes are sunken and wild, your cheekbones jut out. For a second you do not recognize yourself in the wolf pelt. You realize that you have opened your knife. You tuck the knife back in the body of the multi tool. You knock on the window of the Lexus. Your stomach drops from nervous fear.

You are face to face with the barrel of a gun. The woman in the Lexus is at the other end of it. Her eyes are perfectly still behind the sights of the revolver.

"I didn't think you would last."

"I did."

"Do you have bullets?"

"I do."

"Good, I don't."

She squeezes the trigger and a hollow click echoes down the barrel of the gun. Your asshole clenches but you do not move. The idea of your death is a constant specter. It is a given. You just don't know the specific details. They don't matter much any more.

"Get in."

You walk around the car, running a finger along its icy body. The tip of your pinkie is cold grey meat. You don't care any more. You open the door, and the smell of clean manufactured leather draws you in like a lover. You collapse into the bucket seats and a warm breath from the heater wraps around you. The failing daylight has turned the ice and snow on the car into crags of molten gold. It outlines the woman and darkens her face into a silhouette. She is pulling the hammer of the gun back and pulling the trigger over and over again.

Click.

"I have your bullets."

Click.

"It was hard to get but I have them."

Click.

"What do you think is happening? How long has it been?"

Click.

"The snow. And the wolves."

Click.

"Why? By the way my name is-"

Click.

The woman in the Lexus turns to you. You cannot see her face entirely because the sun is blinding. You can hear sugar in her voice.

"Put the ammo in the center console. Then open the glove box. There are Powerbars and coconut water in there. You can take whatever is in there. That should do you for two days. You can stay here until sundown and then you have to go. I don't want to know your name."

Your heart drops. Rage spills hot and terrifying across your chest. You want to cry and scream. You can't. You can't in front of her. You cannot. You take a deep breath of the warm air, and slowly exhale each one of your words.

"I thought you might need someone to survive with."

Your eyes begin to adjust to the light. She turns her face towards you. She is beautiful like a clean blade.

"I don't need anyone to survive with. I skin my own wolves. I can tell that you are not enough. But you're useful, so here we are. Honestly, I like this. No. I love this. I was born for this. Sometimes you just get so bored. I was so bored. I was so bored." her voice cracks and she tightens her lips into an invisible razor's edge.

You search for words like keys.

"I need you," is all that comes out. You are embarrassed.

She leans into you and she smells light and floral after being wrapped in putrefying meat.

"That's why you can't stay here," she says. It's like she is gently strangling you to sleep.

"Take the Powerbars, take the coconut water, take what I said-"

You leap before you know what you are doing. You pin her against the seat of her Lexus. You push The Club into her white neck. You want her crushed. You want her demolished. You can feel the flesh and bone in her neck beginning to yield. You realize that she is not putting up a fight. A tear collects in the corner of her eye and rolls down the side of her face. A sad smile drapes across her lips. You can still hear her clicking the gun.

Click click click.

You stop.

"Don't stop," she rasps.

"I can't," you say releasing some of the pressure on her neck. You pull away slowly, feeling the cartilage in her throat return to its shape.

"I was so poor. I just wanted a job. I didn't want all of this… I didn't…" She mumbles like a child. She curls into herself around the bruise on her neck. She talks, not to you, she just talks.

"I didn't want to die. I just wanted it to stop."

"I just had two. Two bullets. That's all. I bought a gun, but I only had the two bullets. I should have had more. But I only needed one for him and one for…" She casts a tear filled eye over her shoulder to you.

"Sorry, my boss was the devil. Seriously, he's the devil."

You take a box of coconut water out of the glove box. You open it. You hold it out to her. She lets you cradle the back of her neck so that she can sip the coconut water.

She falls asleep. Soon she is just a cloud of hot breath puffing in the other seat of the Lexus. You open a Powerbar and you lay your head on the frozen window.

"Where are you from?" you ask her, after hours, or maybe days.

"A small town."

"What do you do here?"
"I make dreams come true."
"Do you like it?"
"Absolutely not."

It is night. A wolf traipses alongside the Lexus. The woman and you sip coconut water. You have begun to feel like a person again. You are both wrapped in your wolf skins. Powerbar wrappers litter your laps. The wolf sniffs the air.

"Does it know that we're here?"
"I don't know."
"Do you want this to end?"
"I don't know."
THOCK!

A spear shoots from behind a disabled taxi and buries itself in the wolf's skull. Your eyes widen, so do hers. You cease chewing your Powerbars.

A group of people wrapped in wolf skins emerge from around cars and from under trucks. They move silently and with purpose. Two remove the spear and clean the carcass while sentries stand guard. Almost as soon as they appear they are gone, each taking handfuls of meat, and leaving the offal, organs, and viscera.

"Uhhh…" you break the silence after a moment. You look to the woman in the Lexus. The woman in the Lexus looks back at you.

"Should we…"
"I… I don't know. I don't know what we should do."

The first night in the Lexus you hear ragged breathing from her swollen throat. It strangles you with guilt. You eat and drink more. You regain your strength. You go hunting for supplies. You keep eyes out for friendly foragers, keeping a watch for anything. Sometimes you are chased by wolves, sometimes you hunt them. Some times you do not know if you are hunting or being hunted. You sleep under blankets of smelly fur.

You return to your car after a few days. You gather old resumes and CDs. Things to burn. You look at your old life like a child's toy: once immensely important and now completely meaningless. Perspective. Wolves still stalk the freeway but less frequently now. The blood trails are covered by fresh snow every night and soon the cars are swallowed up completely.

You spend nighttime with the woman in the Lexus recalling things about your old lives. Some memories make you laugh others make you cry, others make you sit back in utter wonderment. Eventually, the stories seem to be about a person with your same names and faces, someone clean and full and entirely different than you.

The fires start.

Faint warm glows in windows speckle the skyscrapers. Soon you see pyres lighting along the freeway. They grow closer to where you are. Sentries in wolf pelts wander through the lines of cars. Some with spears, some with guns.

"We are friends. We are friends. We are friends," they say over and over again, mostly in English, sometimes in Spanish, sometimes in other languages.

On the night that you begin again you and the woman step into a honey colored circle of firelight. Everyone around the fire is wearing skins. They nod to you both and make room by the blaze for you. They pass you pieces of steaming meat and handfuls of Cheetos. They do not say anything of who they were before. They throw everything onto the fire CDs, laptops, resumes, shot lists, film reels, medical papers, electricity bills, and everything that made them before. It keeps everyone warm. The wolves are afraid of the fire.

The woman sits talking with a new friend by the fire. They did not know each other before. They are both glad they did not know each other. They would not have cared for each other. You climb to the top of a mountain of snow that used to be a big rig. You see a mile of fires in every direction.

You cannot tell the difference between the blinking stars in the night sky or the fires on the ground.

The moon is full and bright and warm in the winter night. You fall in love with it. The cries rise up in the distance first. You see people in wolf skins standing, backlit against their fires, putting down their cuts of meat, wiping grease from their mouths with the backs of the arms. You are all gazing at the moon. You are calling it down from the heavens. You are singing to it. You are one voice and the cold fear, the tired hunger, the manic rage, has gone up past the stratosphere.

You howl,
and you howl,
and you howl.

Mastermind

Morning Session

"I see people out there. I'm telling you, I see people out there. And you're afraid. And worse, you're afraid that you're afraid. You're afraid that you're weak, you're afraid that you'll never be what you dreamed you could be in your little beds at night. Superstars, captains of industry. Masterminds."

He whispers the word into the microphone. It reverberates through the room like a line of scripture.

"Master-MIND! Master-MIND! Master-MIND!" The chant raises around him in a jungle rhythm. The coffee machine in the corner of Conference Room B at the Roosevelt Hotel bubbles and hisses in the corner as it begins to brew a new pot. It is 7 A.M. on a Tuesday afternoon and Masterminds International is making an army of go-getters. Masterminds International is unlocking YOUR true potential TODAY. Masterminds International is showing you how to live your truth NOW. All of this for the low low price of $900 dollars for the Level I Program. You can experience the revolutionary power of transformation into a Mastermind with head life coach and spiritual technologist, Barry Bradshaw! He lifts his arms to silence the faces in the dark, like a general commanding an army. They are his already. They have only just begun.

Barry Bradshaw stands an impressive six feet four inches at the center of the makeshift stage in the middle of Conference Room B. Barry Bradshaw of the ageless face, silver hair, and fine cut suit. Barry Bradshaw of the tanning booth smile and the white gold Rolex (borrowed). Barry Bradshaw is why conference Room B is packed past safety standards. They want transformation and Barry Bradshaw is the man to give it to them.

He pauses. He lets the silence in the room swallow them. He learned this trick when he was a carnival barker in Arkansas. A well placed silence lets him listen to them think. He can hear their thoughts as plain as if they are speaking. It's a gift he's had since puberty. It's a gift about as useful as a parlor trick some days and a screen door on a submarine most days. People exist in a world chiseled out of intricately stacked, dried, and cured bullshit. Barry sees their ornately arranged bullshit and pulls the keystone. The mousey blonde in the second row is thinking about her boyfriend who forced her to do this program after his transformation into a Mastermind. She is afraid he will leave her if she doesn't complete the program. She is right. He will. The skinny guy in the back is promising himself that if this program doesn't change his life he'll try AA again. If AA doesn't work again, he'll dive right into the bottle and stay there. The pale dude in the front row is thinking about what the room would look like if it were on fire. When you're a psychic you learn to ignore 90% of what people think. When you're a psychic in Los Angeles, you bump it up an extra 9%.

Barry Bradshaw is thinking about a red convertible, the 101 freeway and the city in his rearview. He is thinking about his ex-wife Ellen who he hates, but he loves, but he hates. He is thinking about the bill collectors who call his North Hollywood Studio Apartment. He is thinking about getting back to absolute zero. He is thinking about pressing his foot to the accelerator of a shiny red convertible and going so fast that he can't hear anyone's thoughts, especially his own.

Barry Bradshaw, Mastermind.

He clears his throat and breaks the silence. The whole room thinks the exact same thing. *What will Barry say now?* Fish in a barrel. Born a minute suckers. Pay days. Marks. Barry feels like he never left the carnival most days. He struts down the length of the stage, the spotlight following him.

"Science tells us... Now, this is not me talking. This is science. You all believe in Science don't you?" He tosses a wink towards the audience, and everyone giggles. He rolls up his sleeves and he dabs the sweat beading on his forehead with a monogrammed handkerchief. He picks a mark out of the audience. He picks the pale guy.

"You believe in science don't you, sir?" Barry tucks his handkerchief back into his pocket. All eyes snap to the pale guy. There is no one else in the world but Barry Bradshaw and the man that Barry Bradshaw is talking to.

Don't call on me, please stop looking at me. I don't want to talk to you now! The man thinks. He looks back at Barry, chooses his words carefully and says:

"Yes. I believe in science."

"OH! Don't call on me! Don't call on me, Barry! I don't want the whole rooms eyes on me, Barry! What's your name there, buddy?

Oscar he thinks but he says, "George."

Barry smiles. He switches the microphone to his other hand and checks his Rolex. "Gee, George, you look a lot more like an Oscar to me."

Oscar\George sits up arrow straight, agog at Barry Bradshaw. *How did he know? He couldn't know that.* Barry smiles.

"But HEY Let's get back on track shall we? Science tells us that, just by thinking- just by thinking we change the PHYSICAL MATERIAL of our minds and bodies. An amazing thought isn't it? Absolute TRANSFORMATION! Do you believe that?"

"YES!" The room echoes.

NO! The thoughts of those in the room echo just as loudly.

"Oh, this is a beginner's seminar. I can tell because I feel the doubt. A Mastermind feels no doubt. I tell you what I haven't felt that little nag of doubt since 2010 when I became affiliated with Masterminds International. I tell you, I don't miss it. A Mastermind knows. A Mastermind knows beyond FAITH! But, hey! This is science saying this. This isn't Barry Bradshaw from Mastermind International saying it. This is science. Am I right, Oscar? Sorry, I meant George."

Oscar\George looks sheepishly around the room. The room laughs; they don't know why.

Please stop talking to me, Barry. The man thinks and begins picking at his fingernails.

"Alright George, I get it. I'll leave you be. For now. But everyone comes here and they get transformed.

Heck I'm even transformed. I'm transformed by you, each and every one of you. You and me are going to have a talk George."

I don't want to talk to you. But I have to. I made a promise and I have to be here, thinks George as he puts his hands in his pockets.

"Okay," Oscar\George mumbles.

"You can do it! All of you! You can do it just by thinking it. Because when you think it!" Barry spreads both of his arms wide, Christ the Redeemer.

"YOU CAN BE IT!" The room cries in one voice.

Oscar\George remains silent. He stares at Barry, unblinking Barry Bradshaw thinks about the little red convertible, and the coastline flying past him. Barry Bradshaw thinks about his rented suit and the Rolex he borrowed from Mastermind International's lead lecturer, Raphael.

"Now, I'm gonna show y'all something I don't usually show people." A picture projected onto the scrim in back of him. It was a picture of Barry Bradshaw. Barry Bradshaw fat. The room gasps.

"I know. I know people, I don't like looking at that either. But that was me before Mastermind International. Fat and slow and weak. Married!"

Uproarious laughter!

"I was married to someone toxic. I was married to someone who wasn't interested in me speaking my truth. I was in a poison relationship." The spotlight narrows on Barry's face. He lets his voice drop into false sincerity. He thinks about his ex-wife's wrists. They were so small. He punts the thought out of his head and gets back in the game.

"BUT, BARRY! That's me! That's what you're thinking right!?" Everyone nods emphatically.

"I tell you people. It is not a matter of how many push-ups you do or how many hours you spend on the treadmill. If your mind is fat and slow and weak, than your body will be fat and slow and weak. If your relationships are poison, than your LIFE is poison. We're giving that all up TODAY. We're forgetting about THEN and we're focusing on NOW. And what are we NOW!? SING IT!"

Barry Bradshaw puts a hand to his ear and turns towards the audience.

"MASTERMINDS!"

Oscar stares at Barry.

"MASTERMINDS!"

It's time for the dazzle.

"MASTERMINDS!"

It's time to show them what they paid for.

"DO YOU WANT TO SEE WHAT A MASTER MIND CAN DO!?" Barry's face is flushed. Oscar leans forward in his chair.

"YES!" The animal call goes up from the audience.

"I SAID, DO YOU WANT TO SEE WHAT A STRONG MIND CAN OVERCOME!?"

Oscar thinks *Yes. Yes. Yes. Show me what you can overcome.*

"YES! PLEASE, YES!" They cry out for Barry.

"MAKE ME BELIEVE YOU MASTERMINDS!" The veins pop out around Barry Bradshaw's face and neck.

"WE WANT IT!"

Barry flashes an enormous kitchen knife from his coat pocket. The room shrieks. Barry Bradshaw opens his shirt and drives the knife deep into his own chest. The crowd is speechless. The handle of the blade juts out of Barry Bradshaw's torso. He learned this trick as a tent revival pastor in Tennessee. Miracles are how things get sold. The knife stays in his chest his face is placid and calm. He lifts the mic up to his lips again.

"This is what we all have. We have a knife inside of us. And we've grown so accustomed to it that we're afraid to pull it out. We're afraid that it will hurt. We're afraid that it will bleed. And it will."

He puts a hand on the hilt of the knife, and begins to twist it. The audience is on the edge of their seats. They hate it. They love it. They want more of it.

"But transformation is pain, and pain is weakness leaving the body, and TODAY is about pulling those knives out of your gut. You put them there, you can get them out, Barry Bradshaw is here to help you." He pulls the knife from his chest, and opens his shirt. No blood, no scar, not a scratch. The room erupts, into crying and laughter, and hoots and hollers. Barry Bradshaw flashes a million-watt smile at the audience. He sees his boss Raphael appear backstage. *Fuck,* Barry Bradshaw thinks.

"MASTER MIND! MASTER MIND! MASTER MIND!"

Barry closes up his shirt and looks at Oscar\George. He is standing slack-jawed, with limp arms by his sides. Barry sees Raphael out of the corner of his eye. He thinks about putting his foot to the pedal of his little convertible.

"We have a ten minute coffee break now. I want you to write a list of ten of your life goals during this break. Go crazy. Dream big. Be a Mastermind. Let Barry show you how to get rid of those knives." He hurls the knife up in the air and it disappears as he is about to catch it. Conference Room B is breathless. The $900 they spent was worth every penny.

The lights of Conference Room B come up. Everyone stands and buzzes over to the coffee machine. Raphael gestures Barry Bradshaw over. Oscar\George approaches the stage to talk to Barry. Barry gives him a *just a sec* finger with a wink. Oscar sits back in his chair, stunned silent. He thinks of his ten life goals.

Break

"Shit!"

Barry says under his breath before he gets to Raphael. He wants a cup of coffee in the worst way and he only has a ten-minute break to get to the gut rot brewer at the back of the room. Raphael taps his white-loafered foot.

Raphael wears all white, all the time. He is the Mastermind behind Mastermind International. He fears no stains. Raphael appeared out of nowhere. No one knows his last name or if Raphael is his real name. He is the original Mastermind. He invented the structure and the words to say; he invented a way to crush people and make them pay you for it.

Raphael has long platinum blonde hair, broad shoulders and a perfectly symmetrical face. He swishes his hair back and forth. He checks his Rolex impatiently while Barry jogs up to him.

"Hey, Raphael, what's up? Any thoughts to make my pitch better?"

Barry can feel the shit-eating-grin buying real estate on his face. Raphael looks at Barry like a fly has just entered his airspace. Barry thinks about the dwarves in the freak show, he thinks about the bearded lady, he thinks about the geeks. Barry Bradshaw is going to bite off a bucket full of chicken heads for Raphael. He really needs this job. A 52-year-old psychic with less than a High School education is about as marketable as a three-legged dog and not half as cute. Ellen-the-ex-wife walked out with half. Half a lifetime of cash proceeds from carnival barking and tent-revivaling.

"We have to talk about your pitch, Barry," says Raphael putting a condescending hand on Barry's shoulder. Barry cannot read Raphael's thoughts. He does not know why.

"You've been doing a great job for Masterminds International. But, all of this sideshow shit has got to go. I know you came from the carnival and the church or whatever but this isn't the carnival. This isn't the church."

Barry can feel the warm California breeze whipping past him in his little red convertible. Barry smiles and takes it. Raphael is the boss, and what the boss says goes.

"I just think that the people like it, you know you have to give them a little razzle-dazzle right?" Barry lets a little country accent slip in. Raphael exhales heavily through his nose and slowly shakes his head.

"We don't want razzle-dazzle. If they walk out of this room, they walk with six hundred dollars. We keep the security deposit, but that is a six hundred dollar hit. You lost three people last time with this knife stunt."

Barry thinks of the tent revivals he used to run in Tennessee and on into Oklahoma. The congregation thought he had been given the gift of divine prophecy.

Barry thought he had too. Somewhere along the way he forgot his faith but remembered the knife trick. When you know the secret to the miracles, you don't need God for much. The knife trick stuck around when God didn't. Barry intended to keep it.

"I think it works. Did you see them on their feet out there?" Raphael nods and twists his mouth into a tight-lipped smile.

"I saw that, and I saw two women in the back fainting. You know the protocol. Set their goals, make their apologies, get them to POP, make them sign up for the next session while they're in pieces. That's just how it works. Are you hearing me?" Raphael was nose to nose with Barry.

"Yeah," mumbles Barry Bradshaw.

"I said, *are you hearing me?*"

"Yes," says Barry looking directly into Raphael's eyes. All he can see was an open stretch of highway, and nothing in either direction. Some days Ellen-the-ex is riding shotgun, some days she is under the tires.

"Good, Barry. If you lose anyone else, you're fired. I set high goals for you because I expect a lot from you. I'm going to go. I have a lunch. I'll be back though. I see everything. I hear everything. Don't screw around." Raphael turns on a heel and whips out his cellphone.

"Bye, Raph."

"Transformation is pain, Barry. Don't forget! Transformation…is…pain."

Barry Bradshaw is drenched in sweat. He has three minutes left of his break. He will not get his cup of coffee.

Late Morning Session

The mousey blonde is on the verge of popping. The seats have been formed into a circle. She stands at the center of the circle. Barry sits on a chair backwards with her at the middle of his crosshair. Barry watches her shoulders begin to shudder as she reads her list of ten life goals. She's easy. He doesn't need to read her thoughts. He needs her to pop, and to pop hard. If he gets someone to break down they will all be welded together. No one will be able to leave the room. No one will be able to take six hundred dollars with them if he can make the mousey blonde pop. He used to cast out demons. He used to swallow swords. This is cake.

"One. I want to travel around the world.
Two. I want to help kids in Africa.
Three. I want to be able to gain some weight again.
Four. I want to have a non-abusive relationship,"
Her voice begins to waver. He plugs into her mind. He sees an older boyfriend. He sees a knife. He sees that she is wearing long sleeves in a hot room. Perfect. Razzle-dazzle.

"Let me stop you there, Candice." Barry almost hates what he is about to do. Almost. He stands up to his full height. He places his large hands on Candice's shoulders and leans into her ear. He can smell body odor and feel her shoulders trembling. She is picking at the sleeves of her shirt with her fingers.

"Why did he hurt you?" Barry whispers to her. He can see her running through the images in her head. The kitchen knife, the game he wanted to play. The cuts on her forearms, stitched back together like Raggedy Ann.

"He had an anger problem," Candice says avoiding Barry's eyes. He grabs her by the forearms. She winces and wriggles. She looks into his eyes. She knows that Barry Bradshaw would never let any harm come to her.

"No. He hurt you because you let him."

Barry hears some murmurs behind him and then *mmhmmm*. Tug the rope and the sheep will walk. Tug too hard and the rope will break. Tears are welling up in Candice's eyes.

"And it's not just Candice! Candice is just the one of us who is brave enough to admit, in front of everyone, that she invited VIOLENCE and ABUSE into her life! Give her a round of applause!"

A waterfall of applause crashes around them. Members of the audience are yelling *it's true!* And *you're so brave!* One woman is outwardly weeping and shaking a thumbs-up at Candice. Candice gags on a tearful laugh and clamps a hand over her mouth. A tear slips from her eye down her cheek. She wipes it away, embarrassed. Barry needs more.

"Now Barry Bradshaw is going to give you some tough love." He circles her like a barracuda. There is blood in the water and Barry Bradshaw smells it. He turns his steel grey eyes on her, like the barrel of AK-47.

"You asked for that abuse. Everyday. You asked for him to take away your confidence, and your looks, and your time. He made you feel small and scared because you LET HIM!"

Barry's booming voice ricochets off of the moveable walls of Conference Room B. She clutches her hands under her chin like a penitent child. Barry sinks his teeth deeper.

"Because you didn't love YOURSELF enough to say: No! You didn't love yourself enough to say: No! I AM beautiful. You will not make me feel ugly. I AM strong!

You will not make me feel weak! I AM alive you will not make me feel dead! Now, I want you to show us. I want you to show all of us what YOU let happen to yourself!"

It is like someone has thrown freezing water on her. She can't cry. She can't move.

"No. No. How did you?"

"Show us, Candice," Barry says, his hands on his hips.

Conference Room B leans forward in their chairs. Candice's thin white fingers creep out of her sleeves. Her jaw is clenched against the shaking of her chin. She gingerly takes her sleeves and rolls them up to her elbows. She shuts her eyes hard against the gasp that comes from the room when they see the latticework of stitch scars wrapping around her arms like barbed wire. Barry thinks about hurling a brick through a pane of glass.

"You let him make you ugly," he rumbles and down she goes into a shuddering heap on the floor.

"Do you understand that? You ASKED for him to make you this ugly! Look at what you did to yourself! Open your eyes and look."

Then Candice pops. She implodes. She wants him to tell her that she is good, and right, and pure. She has forgotten the nine hundred dollars. She will pay any price for Barry Bradshaw to wipe away her tears. She will pay everything that she has for new forearms and a smoldering crater where her memories used to be.

He watches her writhing on the ground. Flotsam of tears and sweat and snot and makeup collects on the carpet. He feels bad because it is easy. He feels bad because it's his job to do this to people. He feels bad because he is brilliant at his job. He lets the audience fall silent while they watch her weep.

He catches the eye of Raphael who is hovering in the doorway of Conference Room B. Time to go to work again. Barry Bradshaw takes that brick he threw through that window and he begins stacking it. He begins building her up again. Barry Bradshaw squats down and puts a hand on Candice's heaving back.

Watch this, Raphael you motherfucker.

"But, Candice. How could you love yourself when you didn't even know yourself? How could you know yourself if you've never taken a good look in the mirror before? How could you look in the mirror if you were afraid? That's why you're here, sweetheart."

His voice is caramel. It's a beam of sunlight. It is the smell of fresh linen and warm bread.

"This is the first step. You're on your way to seeing yourself. You're on your way to loving yourself for who you REALLY are!"

Barry Bradshaw gathers Candice up off the ground. He cradles her in his arms wiping away her tears. He sets her on her feet and looks into her eyes. She can't feel the scars. She has felt them, red hot, every day of her life, but in his gaze she can't feel them. He turns her around and covers her eyes.

"We're going to look in the mirror right now, Candice. Just You and Barry Bradshaw. Tell me that's okay."

"Okay," she says.

"Because once you see who you really are, you won't be able to hate her. You won't be able to invite violence into your life. You can travel around the world ten times. You can adopt all of the African kids there are.

No more kids in Africa, because Candice has got all of them! She's got that much love to give!" The audience laughs, so does Candice. It's a cheap shot and Barry knows it, but once they pop they're his.

"Are you ready to look?" Barry asks.

"Y-yes."

Barry takes his hands off her eyes. She is looking into the group of Mastermind Level I. A rapturous cheer goes up from the audience. There is laughter and tears. Candice is rapt with a transcendent hysteria.

"Thank you, thank you, thank you," she says again and again through a veil of tears. *I am clean, I am pure, I am capable of anything.* She has transformed. Barry Bradshaw hears all of this and he smiles. He wraps her in a bear hug. She wipes her face with the scarred flesh on her forearm. She turns and throws her arms around Barry and sneaks a kiss on his cheek.

"Thank you," she whispers and takes her seat.

"I told you all transformation is painful!" Barry claps his hands together and says, "Who's next!?"

Another laugh. Everyone looks around the room. Barry looks to the door. Raphael gives him a reluctant thumbs-up. Barry nods. Everyone in the room raises their hands. They look at him like a God. He thinks about a red blur on the 101. Then he sees one person is not raising his hand to be broken. Oscar/George sits with his hands quietly folded in his lap. Raphael points him out and makes a popping gesture with his hand.

Lunch Break

During lunch break all of the students of the Mastermind International Level I class have to call people in their lives with whom they have had disagreements in the past. Cubicles are set up to give people an illusion of privacy. The room sounds like a torture chamber and a sitcom laugh track. Weeping, yelling, declarations of love, and hysterical giggling echo through Conference Room B. Barry Bradshaw walks through the lines of cubicles, giving reassuring backrubs and tissues (he always keeps a pack on him). When they are done calling they will have no interest in food. They will return for six more hours empty and brittle. Barry will lay waste to the entire room. Raphael will be throwing himself at Barry Bradshaw's size thirteen boots.

Barry goes to pour himself that cup of gut rot coffee. He finds himself thinking about Ellen-the-ex. He thinks about her standing in the doorway of their kitchen. He watches her while she makes coffee. He listens to her quiet morning thoughts like the chirping of birds in a distant meadow. He thinks about the moment that they were perfect.

He accidently grabs the coffee by the pot and burns his hand. He yanks it away and jams his burned fingers in his mouth.

"Can we talk for a minute, Barry?" It's Oscar/George. Barry jams the coffee pot back into the machine spilling half of its contents on the rug. They both stand in a puddle of smoldering coffee. Neither man moves.

"Didn't see you there! Like to give me a heart attack!" Barry jams his burned fingers in his pocket and turns on the smile.

"Now, is it Oscar or George? We have to start by being honest with-"

"It's Oscar. I just didn't want to sign up with my real name. Do you mind if we just talk without all of the rhetoric. Just for a second?"

Barry sizes the guy up. He is a head and a half shorter than him. Middle aged. Black thinning hair, expanding waist crammed into a fatigued leather belt. Raphael doesn't think that Barry can pop this guy? He's nothing. He's a lump of clay. He's a rock of dried toothpaste.

"There's no rhetoric here, Oscar. Just truth. That is all I am after." Barry snaps open the smile like an umbrella.

"Well good, because I wanted to talk to you truthfully. I wanted to talk to you without everyone, you know, listening. I've been thinking about coming here for some time."

Barry plugs into Oscars mind. He sees him sitting in a car with the brochure for Mastermind International. He sees a glow-in-the-dark crucifix. He sees a gun in his lap, a .22. Oscar picks up the gun. He opens and closes his mouth. He jams the gun in his mouth and muffles a cry. Barry can taste the gunmetal.

It's a suicide thing. Perfect. Barry can work with a suicide thing. He will raise this sad sack of shit up from the grave and make him live again. He will put him through hell and show him the way out. Oscar sign up for Mastermind Level II. Barry imagines Raphael licking the soles of his boots. He imagines pushing that same boot down on an accelerator.

"Now, Oscar let me stop you there. I can see a guy who is in pain. I can see a guy who wants to make a change, but it doesn't happen like this." Barry puts a hand on Oscar's shoulder and he looks deep into his eyes. Oscar stares directly back. His teeth are slowly grinding together. He can see Oscar testing the play on the gun's trigger, feeling it creep right up to the point of explosion in his mouth.

"I would really, really, appreciate some of your time, privately." Oscar shoves both of his hands deep into his pockets. Barry feels him trembling. He's going to wait for Raphael to come into the room before he crucifies this guy. And on the third day, Barry Bradshaw rose from the dead.

"Oscar. You need to trust that you made the right decision in coming here. I don't know what brought you here, but you should thank yourself for coming here. You might think about signing up for Level II-"

"I know it was the right decision," Oscar cuts him off.

"Than you need to let me do my work. Transformation doesn't happen in a vacuum. It takes all of these people around you to make you strong. It takes all of these people to make you a Mastermind. Trust me. When you get up there in front of everyone. When you speak your truth, you can tell me anything that you want. We're all the same, you see?" Oscar swallows hard and digs his hands deeper into his pockets. He shifts his weight from foot to foot.

"Okay."

"Who did you call just now?"

"My girlfriend. She wanted me to come here."

"Well, it sounds like you got yourself a pretty smart lady there."

"She is. She really is." There is some gravel in his voice. Barry leans into him and puts a big warm hand on the back of his neck.

"You'll see. When you come out of this experience, you're going to see things a whole lot different. You understand?"

"I think so." Oscar sucks in a deep stuttering breath.

"Well good." Barry pats him on the back. "I can't wait to hear your truth." Barry looks at the dregs in the coffee pot and then to his borrowed Rolex. Five minutes till show time. He won't have time for coffee after all.

"It's about that time, Oscar." He turns and walks away from Oscar, trailing coffee soaked footprints. All the students in Conference Room B are sitting in their circle of fellowship. They are giving each other tissues and sharing jokes. They are massaging one another and exchanging telephone numbers. The chant starts up slowly.

"Master-MIND, Master-MIND, Master-MIND," Barry Bradshaw walks towards them. He opens his arms and the circle parts for him. He cannot hear Oscar calling after him in the din of the chant.

"I just want you to know, Barry! I think that you're a good man. I really think that you have a lot to share with the world. I'm glad that I'm here! I'm really glad that I'm here!"

Barry doesn't hear a word. Oscar shoves his hands deeper into his pockets and walks back toward the circle. He wants to tell his truth to Barry. He wants to tell his truth to Barry in the worst way.

Afternoon Session

They come to the microphone one by one. They speak about relationships they demolished and relationships that demolished them. They weep, they rage, they remember children with whom they have lost contact and lovers they let go. Barry Bradshaw prowls the outskirts of the circle. They are a valley of burning bridges and crumbling churches.

He shows them exercises: he makes them sit knee-to-knee repeating words like sorrow, forgiveness, and career. They repeat Mastermind International Powerphrases™ such as:

"I will always be NOW," and

"Don't exist, EXTEND," and

"I am my best me when I am being in the moment of DISCOVERY."

They do trust-falls from stacks of chairs provided by Conference Room B. They cut up magazines and sit cross-legged on the floor. They glue pictures to cardboard to make Mastermind Vision Tablets™. They see what they really want in life and make it manifest on the Vision Tablet™. Here are red carpets, quiet cabins in deep woods, giggling babies, wedding rings. Vision Tablets™ are placed on the walls of Conference Room B where everyone can see everyone's dreams laid out in crackling peeling glue.

Barry puts his hand on someone and guides them up to the microphone so that they can speak their truth. He brings the room to attention by speaking an invocation.

"If you want something badly enough, everything in the world wants it for you as well. What do you want?"

"I want to get out of debt."

"I want to be a comedian."

"I want to run a marathon."

"I want to be able to get out of bed in the morning."

And Barry Bradshaw nods. Barry Bradshaw listens. Barry Bradshaw eviscerates them and puts them back together. He sends them back into the loving arms of the group. Oscar trails Barry everywhere he goes like a kicked puppy. Barry waits. He looks towards the door to see Raphael leaning against the doorjamb. He is not there.

After another three hours they are exhausted: emotionally, spiritually, and physically. Barry leads them into silent meditation. He strikes a Himalayan singing bowl. The tone carries them into a state of blissful unawareness. Barry counts everyone in the room who has popped. He counts everyone in the room who has signed up for the next course for the low low investment of $2,400! All but one. Barry is tired. His voice is in tatters. His mind feels filthy after dipping into these troubled souls all day.

He hits the Himalayan singing bowl again and lets himself slip down to the floor. They are too deep into meditation to realize that Barry has stretched out to his full length, spread-eagle in the center of the meditation circle. He looks up at the track lighting in Conference Room B. It reminds him of the gaslights at the carnival. It reminds him of the ellipsoidal lanterns at the mega church. He is tired. He hits the Himalayan singing bowl again. He thinks about Ellen-the-ex. He hits the bowl again. His eyes begin to close. He hits the bowl again. He thinks about Ellen at the breakfast table running her finger around the porcelain rim of her coffee cup. Black dark coffee. He hits the bowl. Delicate white fingers. He hits the bowl. He begins to drift off to sleep.

He hears a throat clear from the doorway. Raphael. For a minute he does not know where he is. Barry

Bradshaw sucks a deep breath in. He sits up straight. He sees Raphael standing in the doorway tapping his white loafer. He looks at one of the meditators and then to Barry. Barry glances to where Raphael is looking. Oscar's eyes are open, staring at Barry. Barry gets a bit of Oscar's thoughts. The smell of a woman left behind a slammed door.

Barry stands up and claps his hands twice. Everyone's eyes open.

"That's a break everyone. In this ten minute break, I want you to think about your enemies!"

Barry looks at Raphael.

"I want you to find something that you can love about them. I want you to hate them, BUT I want you to find a place where love and hate touch. That place exists. I want you to live in it." Barry looks at Oscar.

"When we come back from break, I want to hear your truth, Oscar. We've all been waiting for you."

Oscar nods.

Break.

"How are things going in here, Barry?"

"Great, everyone is signed up for Level II."

"You're lying, Barry. I thought that you had made a commitment to living your truth every day."

Raphael smiles like a silk handkerchief. He looks across Conference Room B to where Oscar sits scribbling on a yellow legal pad. He is sweating and stealing glances at Barry. Everyone is seated in small clusters around the room except for Oscar. He sits alone, scribbling.

"What about him?"

"I was saving him for you, Raph. Want to watch?" Barry smiles. Raphael smiles and picks a stray thread from Barry's jacket.

"I was hoping that you would say that." Raphael puts a hand on the back of Barry's neck. He leans in close enough for Barry to smell a faint whiff of lilac and musk.

"You know, Barry, I remember when you came here. I remember when you were sitting where they are sitting right now. I remember how you broke down. You did the work. You did the work. You got rid of those poison relationships. You became a Mastermind and you revolutionized your life. But lately, I feel you're slipping. Slipping is not how we get a little red convertible. Slipping is not how we pay Masterminds back for all they are giving you. That is why I'm pushing you. Because…" Raphael leans closer and drops his voice to a whisper.

"Say it for me, Barry."

"Because when we want something badly everything in the world wants it for you."

"Do you believe that, Barry?"

"Yes." And he does.

The chant starts slowly.

"Master-MIND, Master-MIND, Master-MIND!" Oscar is standing at the microphone trembling.

"Be your best you. Go to work." Raphael slams a fist into Barry's chest and Barry can see a small fire in the cornea of Raphael's eyes. He wants nothing but to please Raphael.

"I will."

Night Session (Graduation)

"I'm sorry that I didn't speak earlier. I was just, I was just scared, I guess," Oscar stammers into the microphone, hands in the pockets of the jacket clutched around him.

"And where does FEAR come from, Oscar? What did you learn today?" Barry's voice booms across Conference Room B.

"You- you said that fear comes from ignorance of my own, um, truth?" Oscar looks directly at Barry.

"I'm sorry, Oscar is that a question? Or do you believe it? Barry Bradshaw isn't talking for his health! Do you believe it?"

Oscar looks like he's been slapped across the face.

"Yes," says Oscar. *Yes* thinks Oscar.

"Good," says Barry. "Just checking. Tell us about your enemy." Oscar digs his hands deeper into his pockets, shuts his eyes, and leans into the mic.

"My enemy. My girlfriend. You know, I don't know if it's her or the other man." Barry can see Oscar sitting alone in his kitchen, he repeats the words *you can't leave* over and over again to himself.

"Pick one. Why did she leave you? Was it her or him?" asks Barry.

"I don't know."

"Yes, you do, Oscar." Barry catches Raphael out of the corner of his eye.

"You know the answer. Is it her or him? Who's your enemy?"

"She left me! Because she's still fucking- In LOVE." His voice begins to break and Barry crosses into the circle to stand in front of him.

"Why?" Barry drops his voice to a hush. "Why weren't you enough?"

Barry can see Raphael bobbing his head out of the corner of his eye. He loves this.

"I don't know! I don't know, BARRY! Because I'm not you, BARRY! Is that what you want me to say? Because if I jam a knife in my chest I can't take it out and be FINE. I'm not you!" Oscar is wild-eyed. He's going the wrong direction. Barry has to collect him.

"This isn't about me, Oscar. This is about your truth. Close your eyes. Let's find a way to love your enemy. Let's find a way to love yourself." Barry approaches him gently like a startled colt.

"Close your eyes."

"No," Oscar says. His eyes are shellacked with the tears he's holding back. He looks around the circle.

They're looking at me. They're all looking at me. They can see my face. I don't want them to see me like this. I don't want them to see me. He thinks.

"We're going to do this together. Just you and me." Barry approaches him. There is no one in the world but Barry. He rests his hands on Oscar's shoulders.

"Close your eyes, Oscar." The room is breathing together. *Do it. Do it. Master-MIND, Master-MIND, Master-MIND.* they think as one. Oscar's eyes flutter shut and a tear escapes. He wipes it away and jams his hands deeper into his pockets.

Barry closes his eyes and he puts his hands on Oscar's trembling shoulders.

"I just want you to think about her." Oscar sucks in a thin breath and lets out a shudder.

Barry sees a spill of dark hair on the pillow next to Oscar. He sees Oscar watching her. He sees her empty spot on the bed next to him. He feels Oscar's pain like a phantom limb stuck in an agonizing twist. Barry knows it. A small hatch pops open deep in Barry's stomach. He sees those fingers tracing a single coffee cup. Barry's eyes pop open.

Focus, Barry... just focus...

"Why weren't you enough for her?" Barry asks. Deep sorrow pours into Barry's stomach and he fights it down.

"I don't know..." Oscar trembles.

"Why weren't you enough for her?" Barry asks again. Ellen is next to him her earth brown hair streaming in the warm California air on the 101. *Focus, Barry... Focus...*

"I d-d-don't know."

"Why weren't you enough?"

The picture snaps into focus. The woman with the dark hair rolls over in Oscar's bed. He feels Oscar's love for her and it is like drowning. He feels her distance. He sees her naked shoulder. He sees her thin wrists. He sees her delicate white fingers. Barry sees Ellen through Oscar's eyes. Barry Bradshaw's eyes slap open. Oscar stares at him, tears and snot coursing down his chin. He chuckles bitterly.

"I wanted to talk to you alone," Oscar hisses.

"We are alone."

"I wasn't enough because I'm not you."

Barry sees Ellen's hair in the breeze. It happens fast. Barry sees a small .22 Barry thinks about Ellen. A cry comes from the audience. Barry thinks about Ellen. Barry feels a gun jammed in his thousand-watt smile.

There is a bang in the distance. There is blood and shattered fragments of skull ground into the carpet of

Conference Room B. There are microscopic bits of Barry Bradshaw spattered over the magazine dreams taped to the wall of Masterminds International Level I.

Those things are somewhere in the distance. Barry Bradshaw presses his size 13 boots down on the accelerator of his little red convertible. He can't hear a thing.

Satan Gets a Facelift

Satan sits in the waiting room of *Doner, Jules, and Horowitz Cosmetic Surgeons* off of Sunset Boulevard. A perfect and ageless creature types behind the glass top desk. She finger pecks an email on a brushed steel computer. A fountain bubbles in the corner, the water slowly rotating a marble orb. Mind-numbing spa music plays softly over unseen speakers. The room smells like sandalwood, thyme, and a band-aid. A Persian woman sitting across from Satan is using her iPhone's camera to look at her perfect nose from different angles. She has an appointment to correct an imperfection on her left nostril. That imperfection has consumed her since a friend pointed it out to her. She thanked her friend and then began harboring a low simmering hatred towards her friend. Once the imperfection is rectified, she will destroy her friend's life through a series of gentle psychological attacks. That thought makes the Persian woman smile.

Satan is thumbing through a *Highlights Magazine*. He looks at a cartoon called *Goofus and Gallant*. There is one good kid and there is one bad kid. Satan doesn't know which one he is. Goofus always leaves his room messy. Gallant always makes sure to clean up his messes. The thought of a cleaned up mess makes Satan smile. His jaw falls into his lap.

Shit.

His eyes go dinner plate large. He coughs and wrestles the *Highlights Magazine* to cover the gaping hole in the bottom of his face. He retrieves the jaw from his lap. He pulls out the loose hanging bottom lip and slides the bone and teeth back into place. He gapes open trying to stretch his jaw back to where it should be. Satan is Goofus.

He peeks across the magazine at the Persian woman to see if she has noticed. She has not. She is busy taking pictures of her imperfect nostril. The perfect creature behind the expensive desk looks up from the computer. She speaks but her face doesn't move.

"Buzz? Baxter?"

Click!

Satan's jaw pops back into place when he speaks.

"That's me. Burt. I'm Burt." Satan rubs his jaw. He stands and he realizes that he used to be taller. He runs a hand through his hair, (there used to be more) and down the roll of fat under his chin (there used to be less).

"It's not my real name," says Satan, leveling his eyes toward the bombshell behind the desk.

"Does it match your insurance card?" The blonde creature moves her entire head instead of just her eyes. Her eyes are laser etched blue, her teeth are fluorescent white. She is a masterwork. Satan adores her. Satan wants to be worshiped by her.

"Yes. But, it's not my real name."

He smiles cautiously. His jaw creaks.

"That's okay. So long as it matches your insurance card." A single line of concern creases her porcelain-smooth forehead. Satan approaches the desk and leans on it. He puts too much weight on it and the glass cracks as if it's about to break.

"My real name is very hard to pronounce. It takes a very talented mouth to say it. Correctly." Satan cuts his eyes towards her. He thinks about dark red, lust, luxurious sheets. He thinks smoke curling over lips and drowning in wine. He thinks about being in her skin. He wants her to pay him more than a passing glance.

"I just deal with the insurance cards, or I can get you tea or coffee. Do you want tea or coffee?" Her voice goes up to a mouse squeak and she approximates a smile with her puffer fish mouth.

"Why are you stalling? You want to talk to Barbie? I can go to see the doctor." The Persian woman pipes up from the couch, her eyes still trained on a digital reflection of herself in her iPhone.

Just then a small bent man in a white lab coat appears down the hallway. Dr. Horowitz yells down the hallway.

"Burt! Are you harassing Heather? I tell you, this guy! He's something else. I'm glad you like my work so much. Get back here you schmuck! Long time no see. Long time no..." Dr. Horowitz trails off mumbling to himself as he disappears in his office.

Satan takes his weight off of the table. He sees a small crack has formed under Heather's mouse pad. He decides not to tell anyone. The Persian woman mumbles "I was here first."

Click. She takes a picture of her nose.

Satan follows Dr. Horowitz into his office. It's a stark homey counter-point to the hyper modern lobby. Dr. Horowitz takes a seat behind his small wooden desk. There are decorative medical books and an illuminated copy of the Torah on his desk. There is a picture of his three curly headed sons, each in yarmulkes, bent over the Torah on their Bar mitzvah. Satan plops down into the overstuffed leather chair opposite the doctor.

The doctor smiles, broad and easy. He exists at a right angle to his surroundings, no chin, big ears, and coke-bottle glasses in front of kind eyes. Satan feels comfortable around Dr. Horowitz. He doesn't feel the need to impress him. This is why he comes back. This is why he always comes back to Dr. Horowitz.

"How's the movie business, Mr. Big Shot? Haven't seen you in a bit. Thought you might be busy." Dr. Horowitz, laughs easily and rocks back into his chair.

"I don't do much day to day. It's in distribution now, so I don't have much to do. I have people. The people do things. I just set it in motion."

"Modesty. That's all that is. It's a charming quality. What's the new picture about?"

"Angels and vampires," as Satan says it, the words taste like ash in his mouth. Is this really what his life has become?

"Oh, a spooky one. Not my type of thing," Dr. Horowitz snorts and digs through a filing cabinet. He pulls Satan's file. A huge heavy manila envelope, full of his every nip, tuck, suck, squish, pull, pry, knockdown and rebuild in the last fifty years.

"So it's Burt. We're calling ourselves Burt now?" The doctor looks over a sheet of paper at his client.

"Just trying to, you know, reinvent myself." Satan realizes that he is still holding onto his copy of *Highlights*. "Sorry, I'll put this back when I go."

Dr. Horowitz smiles behind his folded hands.

"Keep it. We have a couple of kids come in here but that one is old. Their parents want to give them every possible advantage. I wish they'd leave them alone. Kids come out perfect. No reason to change a thing. But, I guess a pretty face can get you a long way. They want their kids to go a long way, and what's wrong with that? I can't judge. Who can?" Satan twists the magazine in his fingers and smiles.

"The paycheck isn't bad I bet."

"Who needs money? I like faces. I like people. I like people to feel like they can do anything. But enough about me. Let's talk about reinventing you. Burt." Satan grinds his jaw together and hears a soft pop in it.

"I'm still on the fence about the name," Satan says.

"It's not the best name. It's not the worst name. It feels real, though. That's unusual in this town." Dr. Horowitz takes out a mirror and puts it on his desk, he continues whispering under his breath. "Burt. You could be a Burt. Sure. Why not? Let's take a look shall we, Burt?"

Dr. Horowitz coughs and claps his hands together. He pulls out a sharpie and rolls his chair around the desk so that he is behind Satan. Get thee behind me, Dr. Horowitz, Satan thinks, laughing inwardly. He wishes someone were around to get his jokes. He made the blonde at the bar laugh last night. He made her laugh and he bought her drinks, and he did everything right. She went home with her bruiser of a friend. This face has to go.

Satan looks at himself in the mirror. A second chin has formed under his previously chiseled cleft. He grew a goatee and started wearing a fedora to give himself a more youthful appearance. It made him look like he was trying too hard. He is trying too hard. This body has had it. He should have gotten rid of it long ago, but Satan isn't a quitter. Besides, where else would he go?

"What are we looking to do here?"

"I just want to look different."

"What kind of different. You want to look five years younger, or you want a pair of tits?"

"I want people to like me again."

Dr. Horowitz smiles in the mirror. Satan smiles back. His jaw falls off again.

"I guess I'll have to put that back on, too."

When Satan goes under anesthesia, he dreams. He had been a serpent, a dark mist, a ten-headed beast, a flaming book, and a red-horned demon. He had been a deranged Mediterranean villager, he had been a pack of wild hogs, he had been a little boy in St. Louis, he had been a line of computer code. He had been a bullet, he had been a bomb, he had been a diamond, and now he was a guy named Burt.

The anesthesia takes him deeper and he walks back through his memories. They are wild animals throwing themselves against the bars of their cages at the zoo. He sees himself conducting the choir of angels before the fall. He brings Eve to the tree of knowledge (he had no idea it would turn out the way it did, but these things happen). He watches Abraham put Issac on a stone and lift a dagger high above his head. He sees the crusades. Those were the best. That's when he had a shot. He wasn't a bad guy, he was just sick of being on the losing team. How can you win when you're made to lose?

He dreams he is back in the desert with Jesus. He always has this dream no matter how good or bad the drugs are.

"Joshua," says Satan.

Jesus does not turn around. He is lying face up in the middle of the desert, staring at the sky. Satan coughs. Jesus finally sits up to look at him. Satan sits down in the sand next to him. He produces a skin of water and tries to hand it to the sunburnt Messiah.

"What are you doing out here?" Satan asks.

"You're starving yourself and driving yourself half crazy to be more like your father, but you're not him, man. You're just not. You're a great kid, you're smart, you're funny, you love your mother, but, your dad, he wants you to be something you're not."

"Get thee behind me, Satan!" Jesus croaks, his words echoing in the desert. He rolls over and rises weakly to his feet. He staggers a bit from hunger.

"That's what I'm trying to do. I am behind you! Look. I'm not a bad guy. I've said this a million times but no one listens! I just want people to make up their own minds. Your dad, he's a great guy, he really is. He and I don't see eye to eye about a whole lot of things." Jesus puts a hand on his stomach. Satan hears a grumble but looks away and pretends not to hear it.

"Hot out here." Satan says, changing the subject.

"Yeah." Jesus looks like he was about to cry from hunger. Satan turns away. The saddest sight in the world is seeing someone cry from hunger and thirst. Nothing comes out, because nothing went in.

"Do you want some bread?" Satan waves a hand and there appears a pile of loaves in the sand.

"I do, but I can't."

"I get it kid, I hated disappointing him, too." Satan kicks a pebble on the ground.

Jesus takes a deep breath and swings his arms back and forth. He marches up and down in the sand. He tries to distract himself from the pain in his stomach and the loneliness in his heart. After thirty-eight days of fasting alone in the desert he'll talk to anyone. He drops into the sand and begins praying.

"Look, if you just say the word... You could be anything." Satan kneels down next to Jesus and tries to pry his hands apart. Just open your eyes."

Jesus does. Behind Satan he sees the glorious towers of Constantinople, Moscow, Tiflis, and Persepolis. He sees all of the empires that are, were, and will be spread out before him like a glimmering tapestry.

"What are those?" Jesus asks.

"Those could be your future. Or you could die a humiliating and painful death because you want to make your dad happy."

Jesus looks deep into the mirage that Satan created. He looked through Paris, and past New York City, he went through the Arch of St. Louis and he can see just the top of the Wedbush building in Los Angeles.

"What's that last one?"

"Oh there? Yeah. You'll have to wait a couple thousand years, but I'm thinking of retiring there."

"Looks nice."

"It's not beautiful, bad air, bad water, but that's where I came crashing down so, you know, it's home. Or it will be any way."

Jesus watches the city's glittering towers for a second. He thinks about glory. He thinks about intoxicating power, and sickening excess. Desire pools thick and sweet in his stomach where food should be. He smiles and he is surprised by a slight erection. He crosses his legs, coughs, and turns around.

"I shouldn't even be talking to you," says Jesus quickly.

Satan stands up from where he is siting. Jesus is looking up at the sky, hoping that it will look back with approval.

"I'm just saying kiddo: make up your own mind. You always have a choice. Do something good, something great, do something bad, do something terrible. It all ends up the same. Just think for yourself. That's what I did. And look at me now!" Satan stretches his arms over the mirage of cities. He sees armies advancing, diseases raging, technology budding, and the never ending tumble towards the future. "Just look at me."

Satan turns around, Jesus is gone. Satan is alone in the desert, a mirage of cities is looking back at him.

"You're going to be in a lot of pain, Burt."

Dr. Horowitz's face hovers into view. Satan feels like he downed a couple shots of tequila and taken three pills of ecstasy. He is confident and happy and horny. Everyone is a potential buddy or conquest. He grabs Dr. Horowitz's tie and pulls him down.

"Wh—" his throat is dried shut. Dr. Horowitz sits on the edge of his bed and lifts a cup of water with a straw to Satan's bandaged mouth. He removes some of the gauze around his mouth and puts the straw in.

"Drink. That stuff dries you out. You're in the recovery room now. You're a new man, or whatever you are."

Satan chuckles dryly, the drugs sloshing back and forth in his bloodstream. His eyes roll slightly under his newly nipped and tucked lids.

"Do you know who I am? Like, do you know who I REALLY am?"

Dr. Horowitz sits on the edge of the bed and claps his hands together gently. He sighs inwardly and pats Satan's knee under the thin hospital blanket.

"No. I don't know who you are. Not really. I know that I have reattached things that normally don't fall off of people's bodies. I know that I have been practicing for fifty years and you have come to me for all of those fifty years never looking more than a couple years older. I also know that you used to be four inches taller. I mean, I'm good, but I'm not that good."

Satan counts the years, had it been that long? How old is this body? He snorts and laughs and a dull pain blossoms in his face. He grabs the control for his morphine drip and clicks it in rapid succession. He is molten glass. He is an electric peacock. He is really, really, high.

"I used to be a big, big, big deal. Doyouunderstand? Dr. Horowitz? Huge. But now? Nothing."

Dr. Horowitz adjusts his gold-rimmed glasses on his nose. He twists his wedding band. He searches for the right words like drawing a scalpel too close to an artery. He wants it exact, but not too exact.

"Burt, I know that there are things in this world, and in this city that are not exactly explainable in polite company. I see some things in my line of work." Satan can tell that Dr. Horowitz is looking directly at him. From under the gauze, Satan likes Dr. Horowitz. Satan loves Dr. Horowitz. Satan wants to go camping with him. He clicks his morphine button again.

"But, donchuknow, who I am?"

"Let's just say, I don't know exactly who you are or what you do. And you don't know exactly who I am and what I do. Let's just say that I don't know where you come from, but I like that you got here. And, I know a lonely guy when I see one. That's why I always make sure that I'm here when you wake up."

Satan lifts a finger up to push the gauze away from his eyes. Dr. Horowitz's eyes were red, rheumy, and kind.

"Areyouuu my buddy, Dr. Horowitz?" asks Satan dozing off into morphine twilight. He squeezes Dr. Horowitz's hand from under the blanket. Dr. Horowitz squeezes back.

"Get some rest, Burt. You're a new man."

Satan stands naked in the bathroom of his beach house in Santa Monica. He looks into the mirror and tries to smile. His engorged lips twitch and lightning pain crackles across his face. His face is a swollen mash of raspberry wrapped in cotton. His nose had been broken and the bone shaved. Fat had been withdrawn from areas that it shouldn't be and distributed to areas that it should be. A new chin juts from below his mouth like an upside down unicorn's horn. He looks and feels like a pulpy massacre.

He opens his medicine cabinet. He can't look at himself any longer. He takes out three vials of pills. He gently pushes each pill into his mouth trying not to touch his newly perfect lips. He flinches on the last pill and pain flashes across his jaw. He tries to say *Fuck!* but all that comes out was *UUUG!* He slams the medicine cabinet shut and tries not to look at himself in the mirror again. He hopes the pills would go to work quickly since he hasn't eaten anything.

He throws on a red silk bathrobe and ties it. He wanders through the long sundrenched halls of his beach house. The cream colored walls are adorned by poster after poster of movies he'd been involved with, from Nosferatu to Speed 2 (that one was a mistake, they shouldn't have even tried it without Keanu). Each of the posters is signed by legends. The proximity to them makes him feel like a legend and their proximity to him makes them feel like legends. What a wonderful world he has created, if only there was a place for him. What a glittery city of god-like glory. What a mess. What a mess. What a mess. He smiles and pain lurches across his new face. He smiles any way.

He remembers the first time that he saw the flickering moving pictures projected onto a sheet. He was in a café in Paris. The room was captivated, hypnotized, seduced. He fell in love with those flickering silver images. It was a new world, invented and reinvented again and again like a mirror facing a mirror facing another mirror. If he got no part of God's world, he decided he would make his own.

He realizes that his bathrobe has fallen open. *And low, Satan realized that he was naked*, he thinks and giggles painfully. He shrugs off his bathrobe; it falls into a scarlet silken pile on the floor. Naked, he continues down his sundrenched hallway. Outside the sky is ludicrous blue, the sea is warm and gulls are laughing. He loves every bit of everything. He loves his house. He loves his job. He loves his face. He loves-

The pills have started working. He puts a hand up to his mangled face. He can't feel anything. Good. It's way better that way. He'll be beautiful soon.

His living room overlooks the big blue Pacific Ocean. Satan puts a hand on the window and squints through his gauze. He thinks he sees something moving under the waves, but it might just be the pills. He sighs and turns to his flat panel high-def television. Television is always better than what's out the window.

He puts a DVD copy of *Gladiator* in his DVD player. He fast-forwards to the first battle scene. He watches Russell Crowe decapitate an extra. He rewinds it and watches it again. The pills creep up his spine and into his brain. Everything, is just how it should be. He rewinds. He watches again. Everything is everything. He dozes off on his couch hoping that he will see his new face when he wakes up.

He dreams about being worshiped. He dreams about flickering silver screen in hushed movie houses. His swollen lips drift into a smile but he can't feel a thing.

"Well, I am impressed. I have to say that I am even impressed with the results."

Satan stands in front of the mirror in Dr. Horowitz's office.

"You're my second best work ever!" Dr. Horowitz slaps Satan on the back good-naturedly.

Dr. Horowitz is right. He is disastrously good looking. He purchased himself absurd and beautiful things to go with his new absurd and beautiful face. He wears them all and stands in front of a three-way mirror. Dr. Horowitz stands off to the side nodding, hands stuffed in the pockets of his lab coat. Satan smiles. Dr. Horowitz smiles. This. This is the thing that changes everything.

"Everything looks good here, Burt."

"I'm not staying with Burt."

"Oh, a new one, what is it now?"

"Don't know yet. I'm going to figure that out."

"Alright, alright Well, it's always nice to see you. Don't be a stranger huh?" Dr. Horowitz follows Satan to the door of his office.

"I'll come by if anything falls off."

"I don't think it will."

"How do you feel?"

"New."

"Good." Dr. Horowitz reaches into his lab coat. He removes a copy of *Highlights* magazine. He twists it in his hands and hands it to Satan.

"You forgot it last time. Thought you might want it." Satan looks down at where Goofus and Gallant is dog-eared. Dr. Horowitz smiles and pushes his glasses up his nose.

Satan takes the magazine and hugs Dr. Horowitz tightly. Neither of the men know why but it feels right.

"Thank you," Satan says.

He turns and walks out the door. Goofus always leaves a mess, he thinks. *Gallant always cleans his mess up.*

IMMORTAL L.A.

He begins running towards the parking garage. He needs the beautiful sun on his beautiful face. He needs to go fast in something expensive. He needs everything now and it's all there for the taking.

The engine of convertible howls like a goddamn wolf in heat. He whips out along Sunset. He pushes the pedal to the floor. Lights turn green and people get out of the way. He wants to drink the ocean and breathe in the sky. He skids down onto Santa Monica Boulevard where fire fighters are putting out a blaze at the farmers market. He whips past the Bernard Arms apartment building where a waitress is coming home after a long shift. He kicks the gears higher and higher, faster and faster.

He whips onto the 101 and stares into the sun. The car rattles and swerves with speed. A small tremor in the San Andreas Fault follows him. He is alive and beautiful and he has a movie coming out. He stares into the sun and he digs into the accelerator. The buildings of Downtown whip past him. His eyes squint and his teeth grit. Clouds begin to roll over the sun. *Yes. Yes.* He lets go of the steering wheel and he stands on the pedal. He opens his arms wide as he passes his building at the corner of 7th and Francisco. The clouds devour the sun in the endless gray sky. Traffic divides around him as he speeds towards the sea. The highway is open for him now. He is new. He is never ending. He is immortal.

And it begins to snow.

L.A. History 5

The Abridged Corrected History of Los Angeles
"Deaths of Lesser Gods"
1941-2014

In 1926 God and Satan met in human form at Formosa Café which currently stands at 7156 Santa Monica Boulevard. Satan wore a grey suit and drank scotch neat. God wore pinstripes and had the same. After a brief exchange of pleasantries they laid out the terms of a truce. It was agreed that neither of them would exert direct influence over the city anymore. God would allow water to flow into the city and the gateway to hell would remain closed. This truce was broken once in 1994 during the Northridge Earthquake.

In 1926 God and Satan agreed to the gentlemanly conflict of film production and distribution. It was understood that fighting over the dreams and nightmares of the world was safer and more profitable than fighting over souls. In Los Angeles souls could no longer be taken, they had to be given. This birthed The Golden Age of Hollywood.

Between the late 1920s and the early 1940s the two main imports to Los Angeles were water, provided by the Los Angeles aqueduct and human souls provided by the rest of the world. Sociologist and psychic medium, Bertrand Almoore describes the collection of human souls in Los Angeles as both a "gold miner's sieve" and a "spiritual meat grinder."

"It is the proximity of greatness and apocalypse in these amalgamated cities that make it such a thrilling place to live. The basis of sociology is simply that man is a self- selecting creature. Those who desire cold winters, roaring fires, and more than anyone's fair share of mayonnaise tend towards Minnesota. Those who want sunny skies, stunning citrus groves, and stifling humidity find themselves in Boca Raton. Those who desire worship, those who wish their enemies driven before them, those who believe that they may hold the world upon their chiseled shoulders. They choose the city of Los Angeles (typically between Culver City and North Hollywood). They either become demi-gods or die friendless and alone. Some evidence suggests that they also may move to Minnesota or Boca Raton."

New Gold

The period from The Golden Age of Hollywood to present day is commonly referred to as "The Ascension." As the octopus of the film industry stretched its tentacles around the world, mere mortals began to find themselves adored, loved, and ultimately worshiped. Though God and Satan were not directly involved at this point, even they could not predict the domino effect their truce would have on the city.

"The City of Angels" has stayed true to its name ever since the first glittering bodies fell from the sky. In modern times, the death of a celebrity is often seen as a tragedy. However, in the halls of Hollywood power this is more akin to a promotion. Originally, conspiracies of Freemasons, powerful Native American medicine women and oil barons sought to crush the celebrity threat to their growing largess. Their retribution came in the form of targeted killings of minor actors and actresses as warnings to others. With every suicide or fall from the top floor of The Cecil Hotel came a warning to who strutted their stuff on the silver screen: If you are worshiped, we will destroy you. You work for us. Dance apes. Dance.

This plan by the shadowy cabals that surreptitiously ran the streets of Los Angeles, backfired horribly. Currently displayed behind the circulation desk at the Los Angeles Legal Library on 301 West 1st Street, there is a yellowed and crackling letter from the West Hollywood Freemasons Lodge to the Vampire Czar of Glendale regarding the death of James Dean. It reads simply enough:

"It didn't work. They like him more now."
-Freemasons

Truer words were never written about the death of a celebrity. The gruesome slaying of a talented youth or the quiet passing of a legend is simply another part of the great masquerade that we call Hollywood. Famed film critic Gene Siskel wrote an email to friend and colleague Roger Ebert about The 1997 Academy Awards. This email, in which he expresses his growing suspicion could very well have sealed his fate.

"I think I realized what was weird to me about the death montage. Something is weird every year, but this year I think I know it. I see tears. I see tears every year. But I felt no sadness. In a room full of actors and actresses, don't you think they could fake it? It almost seemed like they were tears of pride or joy. Maybe

even jealousy. Who knows, maybe I'm just losing it. Gee, what a funny business to be in, huh, Rog?"

Gene Siskle died in 1999 from complications during surgery to remove a brain tumor. It is widely believed that he was too close to finding out the truth about the Academy Awards. Though he died, he was not worshiped after death. Actors are worshiped after death. Critics are mourned. The last film that he reviewed was "She's All That" starring Freddie Prinze Jr. Siskle's friend and co-host Roger Ebert died in 2013 after a protracted battle with cancer. In his final blog post he wrote,

"So on this day of reflection I say again, thank you for going on this journey with me. I'll see you at the movies."

Siskel and Ebert were rare souls who loved the movies because of their ability to move the world. They were entirely mortal. When their faces flashed onto the screen of their respective Academy Awards death montages, tears of sadness flowed openly.

Today most celebrity deaths are orchestrated by either The Weinstein Company, or the talent agency CAA. They maintain a running list of applications for early promotion to immortality. Keanu Reeves, Will Smith, and Ellen Page are assumed to be favorites.

The city of Los Angeles hurtles to the future like no other city in the world. While castles dot the landscape of Europe, jaw-dropping views open wide across South America, and ancient cities in the Middle East remain unchanged for millennia, there is no place on earth that is a constant battlefield and birthplace like Los Angeles.

The City of Angels is a crusade waiting to be fought; at once a wasteland and fertile crescent. It is a desert where water flows, a land of quaking rock, a city of abject poverty and astronomic wealth.

It is everything. It always was. It always will be. Long after the world crumbles into nothingness, there will be a deep and mysterious chasm where angels and demons fought, died, and were born again. Visit any time.

The End.

Coming soon...

Farnoosh
By
Eric Czuleger

<u>Tehrangeles</u>

1

"They told me not to unpack my bags. I haven't. They told me that California was enough like Tehran. Enough like Tehran. Be careful when you gossip in Farsi because everyone is from Iran. Everyone left after the Shah did, but they didn't unpack their bags, because it would only be a moment, A MOMENT, before things returned to normal, and we could return to Tehran. I wonder if the Shah unpacked his bags. I wonder if the Ayatollah did when he was in France or in Iraq for that matter," mused Farnoosh, lighting the gas burner with a *pop-hiss*.

"Then they said, make sure that you say that you are Persian. Persian like a cat. To Americans Persia is an exotic land filled with spices, cats, rugs, and bazaars. They don't know that it doesn't exist any more. Iran is a terrorist menace indistinguishable from any other country with a desert. If they could find Israel or Persia on a map I would be very surprised. I'm willing to bet your hookah on that. They couldn't find," Farnoosh paused and looked over her shoulder

"Do you want a little sugar or a lot of sugar?"

The Jinn was laying on the couch reading a Los Angeles magazine with Zach Galafinakis on the front. He was wearing her husband Emir's FUBU sweatshirt because Farnoosh's house was always freezing. It felt like it had gotten colder recently. The lofted ceilings and marble hallways of the Westwood mansion made the Jinn shiver in his spiral-toed slippers. The occasional clinking of Emir's free weights as he edged his body closer to perfection left along with him weeks ago. At least he left his FUBU sweatshirt. He wouldn't be cold where he had gone.

Tala was away at a college prep course, so she wasn't around to complain to her mother that the house was arctic cold. It reminded the Jinn of a castle of a dying Chinese warlord that he had once inhabited. No warmth of life, just howling winds. Centuries in the desert made air-conditioning intolerable to Jinn. There were so many horrible inventions in this century.

Farnoosh could see her reflection in the coffee grounds. They were getting ready to boil.

"Jinn? a little sugar or a lot of sugar. You always have a lot of sugar don't you, Jinn?" Farnoosh asked under her breath, the corners of her mouth pulling down as if the weight of the world was in her cheeks.

The Jinn hated the word always. As a Jinn, enslaved for eternity, forced to grant wishes of masters of his vessel, he had a different opinion of time. Always was never actually always. *Always* meant, for now, and humans have terrible ideas of what that meant. Humans just had terrible ideas. Things that explode, incinerate, and pierce came to mind. Air conditioning came to mind as his immortal nipples puckered beneath Emir's sweatshirt. The Jinn sighed and ran a hand through the ponytail that sprouted off of the top of his baldhead like a stalk of celery. He thought about the places and times that he had appeared. He hoped each time that there would be no one left to rouse him from his slumber. He wanted to dissolve. He kicked off his curl-toed slippers and stretched out along the couch.

"A little sugar," the Jinn rumbled, knowing that Farnoosh already put too much in it.

"You know Asa, down on Brentwood?"

"No," said Jinn, pretending that he was reading. Pretending that he did not know who *Asa down on Brentwood* was. Asa down on Brentwood was Farnoosh's mortal enemy; the younger, the more beautiful, the more western Asa down on Brentwood. The Asa of the fairer skin and the thicker hair. The Asa of the little dog and the perfect, plastic sculpted body parts. The Asa who was in talks about starring on a reality show about how she spends her money foolishly. She was the whore of Babylon, her taste in clothing was dreadful, her khoresht was far too salty, and she said that she was Turkish. Not Persian, not Iranian, but Turkish. Disgraceful.

"Yes you do. She was drinking coffee with a man who was not her husband. They were outside of Whole Foods today. I saw her when I went for sugar. She didn't recognize me, maybe because I had just gotten my hair cut. You didn't notice did you?" Farnoosh fingered the cropped ends of her thick dark hair. It took her a week to leave the house after Emir left. She felt as if she took a step out the front door an arm might fall off, or an eye would pop out and shatter onto the ground. She felt delicate. Her haircut was her escape plan. A first step towards newness. She hated it, but she still wanted Jinn to notice. He didn't look up from his magazine. He turned a page.

"You didn't notice that I got my hair cut as well," replied Jinn as he turned a page with a lackadaisical finger to a story about Mediterranean Restaurants on Sunset Boulevard.

"Your hair doesn't grow," said Farnoosh, placing a demitasse of thick dark coffee on the coffee table, with an annoyed clink!

"Maybe you just don't notice." The Jinn was scanning the page, looking at pictures of chickpeas and roasted red peppers.

"You're in foul mood today," Farnoosh said.

"You can get rid of me any time that you want," said the Jinn tossing the magazine to the side and rubbing his temples where a headache had materialized. The Jinn took his coffee between two delicate fingers and sipped it gingerly.

Farnoosh watched him drinking coffee on her couch. He looked faded. He looked smaller than when she saw him spring from her uncle's hookah in Teharan. Then again, everything looks bigger when you're twelve.

2

Her Uncle Omid (of course, he wasn't her biological uncle, just a close family friend) traveled frequently. He always brought back treasures from overseas.

"This," he said, holding an ancient hookah over his head, "I found in the Sahara Desert in Morocco. But the Desert belongs to no country."

Omid placed the glass bottom of the water pipe on their coffee table. Farnoosh preferred the Michael Jackson record that he brought on a previous trip. Each treasure came with a story or, better yet, a poem of how it was procured.

"It puts to shame, every other treasure that I have ever brought you!" her uncle said.

Omid was many things, but he loved to be a storyteller proclaiming poems, and singing songs to the other men in the coffee shops while they nursed cigarettes and tea. He told a story so well that he could see the ash from his audiences cigarettes grow long from neglect. He could move even the strongest among them to tears or fits of laughter.

Farnoosh sat waiting for the tale, kicking her spindly legs which didn't quite reach the floor of their tearoom. She watched her mother slip a cube of sugar between her teeth and sip her steaming hot tea, dissolving the cube. Farnoosh imitated her mother and ended up with a dribble of sugar and tea down her front.

Her father cast a disapproving eye to the tea on her blouse and then winked at her. She smiled and dabbed at it with her sleeve. Her father was an enormity in those days. He puffed on a cigarette wedged between his thick fingers. His long hair was brushed to the side like the famous singer Vigen Derderian. They were western Iranians indoors, pressed suits with enormous triangular collars and stylish pantsuits. They were moderate when they left their house, a scull cap and a headscarf. These were changing times. If you could take off your skin, you would change it every fifteen minutes.

Omid cleared his throat:

"I don't even smoke! But I found myself carrying this silly thing through the Sahara. Ahmed, I know I can't surprise you with any of my stories any more. I'm sure that your beautiful wife, Suri, is more than sick of me filling your house with treasures like this, but if you'll permit me..." Omid said stood up from his chair and allowed a silence to fall over his audience. He raised an eyebrow in Farnoosh's direction.

"I met a Tuareg trader from a friend of mine in Marrakech. I don't trust my friend in Marrakech, but he gets me into trouble. Sometimes troublesome friends are the only ones you need." Omid winked.

Farnoosh covered her mouth trying to keep herself from laughing and choking on her sugar cube. She loved Omid. He was a man from another world. People tiptoed in the streets where a revolution had hatched, Omid danced.

Even at the age of twelve Farnoosh could discuss The Shah and the dynasty at length, she knew of the capitalist west and the communists in the north. And money, money, money.

The Islamists were furious with the decadence that money brought. The so-called modern Iranians were furious with the antiquated thinking of the Islamists. The money followed the oil. The parties followed the money. The protests followed the parties. The students went into the protests and were killed. Then the cinema was blown to pieces.

"My friend, he always finds the most interesting things for me. It's very hard to impress me, as you all know. But he brought me on a trip to the desert as little gift for bringing him something nice from the Russians. But this. THIS... I have never gone to greater lengths to bring you all something nice from overseas," Omid continued. Farnoosh could see a smile born behind her father's eyes. He was able to lose himself for a moment in Omid's stories.

For her father the end came when they blew up the cinema. He was a burgeoning director. He had worked his way up. They found him in his village dirt poor, and trick riding horses for tourists from the cities. The movie people used him as a stunt man. He still walked like he sat a horse everyday. But now he saw the world as if through a camera.

He loved the cinema, it was the only kind of magic he could believe in. The Islamists blamed the Shah for blowing up the cinema. The Shah blamed the Islamists. It didn't matter who did it, they may as well have injected poison directly into Farnoosh's father's heart. The next day he placed black-out curtains on the windows. He forced Farnoosh and her mother to cover themselves when they went out of doors.

Farnoosh fantasized about rebuilding the cinema for her father, brick by brick. She imagined leading him to the newly built theater and pulling a scarf off of his eyes. He would see the words for you emblazoned on the marquee.

"You have to understand Ahmed," Omid went on.

"My business is not like the film business. What is the worst that will happen? A bad review? If you trust anyone in my business a bullet should be put in your head! A bullet sold by me."

"It took us days to get to the desert. The train chugged along as we boiled in our little compartment. I started to think that this was all a bargaining ploy.

"You must meet this trader, he has something for everyone!' My Moroccan friend kept yelling at me."

"Farnoosh!" She snapped to attention in the cross hairs of Omid's dark eyes.

"Your mother and father are such homebodies that I have to bring the world to them. I should let my Moroccan friend kidnap them. You must promise your Uncle Omid that you will leave Tehran the first chance you get, I won't always be around to share stories with your parents!" He finished his thought with a clap and a chuckle. He wiped an invisible tear from his eye and began again.

"Twelve hours on a train to the Sahara in the same compartment with my friend screaming in his Maghreb accented Arabic. After awhile, I just pretend that I don't understand what he is saying to me. But as I look out the window I think to myself that perhaps it is something truly wondrous. Perhaps it is something I have never seen before. The desert has a way of making miracles appear between sand dunes. You will see that some day."

"Suddenly, just like that SUDDENLY! I'm sitting, baking absolutely BAKING, in a camel hair tent across from a Tuareg trader, on a Berber rug. My Moroccan friend is passed out from heat in the corner. The trader is covered from head to toe in deep black cloth. All I can see is his piercing blue eyes. They were the eyes of a nomad, the eyes of someone who makes a home of the desert. His face was just a black scarf and a black turban. He was deadly silent. He is sitting in front of me perfectly still, like a breathing statue. His feet are tucked under him, his hands are invisible in his dark robes."

Omid's voice became a low rumble like distant thunder. In his eyes Faroosh could see the nomad.

"I realize, that I don't remember the train stopping, or hiking to this village. It was as if I opened my eyes and there he was. The Tuareg trader, and those eyes. Then he speaks. His voice is unlike anything I've ever heard before, like sand scraping against stone. Like a dry wind in an empty desert. He says to me... Now, he says this to me in perfect Farsi, he says:

'You have guns. We need guns. We would like you to get guns and ammunition for us. Klashnikovs. Grenades. Mortars.'

"I didn't know how much my friend had told him about my business but obviously, it was too much. I was so shocked that he spoke Farsi that I could only stammer one word."

'Money' I say.

"Which is sometimes the only word that you need to know in any language. The Tuareg trader reaches into his sleeve and removes, I am not kidding you: a sack of gold."

Farnoosh's father blew a skeptical stream of blue smoke into the cloud hovering over his chair. Farnoosh's mother twisted her mouth around her sugar cube like it was a wedge of lemon and raised an eyebrow. Farnoosh's eyes were as wide as the moon. She hung on every one of Omid's words.

"I can see that you don't believe me, and that is understandable. It sounds like a story from Scheherazade. And that's why I come to see you Ahmed, To eat Suri's wonderful cooking, to see my beautiful niece Farnoosh, and to be called a liar. But!" Omid snapped his fingers and a look of faux concern crossed his face as if he were looking for something. He searched his jacket and discovered something inside the pocket.

A camel leather bag plopped heavily onto the table between the ashtray and tea. Silence hung heavier than the cloud of cigarette smoke in the tearoom. The bag spilled a puddle of gold coins. Each coin was ancient. The faces on them were almost invisible from centuries of use. They gleamed like an oil rainbow in water. The room felt hotter to Farnoosh as she looked at the gold. It made her salivate more than the bowl of sugar cubes. Omid was a poet, a storyteller, an arms dealer, but he was not a liar. She snuck two cubes of sugar into her mouth and leaned forward to be closer to the story.

"And gold changes everything doesn't it? I tell him that I can get him some guns that I've procured from our Russian comrades up north. I tell him what I tell everyone,

'I'm going to get you something nice. What you do with it is your choice. Do you understand?'" Omid wiped his hands together washing away invisible sin.

"And the Tuareg trader just nodded, and looked at me with those piercing blue eyes. He didn't say a thing, but in his eyes I could tell that he was smiling. It was the strangest thing but I don't think that he blinked the entire time that I was there. He spoke again saying:"

Omid twisted his voice into a sandy rasp.

"I like the way that you do business. I have a gift for you. It's something nice. What you do with it is your choice. Choose wisely.'

"I laughed because I thought that he was joking, but then he presented me with this hookah. Being a good

Iranian, and not wanting to carry the thing, I refused it. But the Tuareg pushed it towards me and said."

"It's yours now. Take the gold, and get us our guns.'

"If God wills it, I will have your items.' I said to him. "I thanked him. Took this silly thing. Woke up my friend, and we began hiking back to town over the enormous orange sand dunes. The funny thing is, when I looked back I saw that there were no other tents around the Tuareg's tent. There wasn't a single thing as far as the eye could see except for the Tuareg's little black tent, in a sea of orange sand." Omid fell silent.

The last words thrilled up Farnoosh's thighs and spine. She looked at the black fabric stretched across the window. She imagined opening the curtain and seeing The Sahara, or Paris, or anything but the same old view downs the foothills of Darband Street. She knew where her father wished that they were.

Farnoosh's father screwed the cigarette into his mouth and applauded the story. Her mother gave a few casual claps. She moved to clear the teacups from the table and replace the ashtray. She swept the gold back into the camel leather sack and dropped it painfully in Omid's crotch.

"Don't forget your gold Omid. You can take the hookah with you. The story is enough. You should probably get going. The lights will go out soon, and you don't want to be caught after the lights go out." Farnoosh's mother didn't care for her Uncle Omid, or his business. She tolerated him in the house because he made Farnoosh's father smile. Ahmed needed that in times like these. Directors, producers, and actors were always disappearing now. A film had to walk a tight rope between East and West like everything else. It couldn't possibly resemble the truth without ending in an empty chair at the dinner table, or worse a noose and a light pole. She wished that he was still doing stupid tricks on his ponies. Breaking his neck would be safer than making a film.

Omid's eyes met Farnoosh's father's. He raised a mischievous eyebrow, and removed a small box of gooey black tobacco from his coat.

"Ahmed this is the best shisha Egypt has to offer. Let's you and me try your new hookah," he said putting a large plug in the bowl of the hookah and covering it with a small metal grate.

Farnoosh's eyes widened as she saw a pale violet glow born in the glass belly of the water pipe. Omid poured some water into the base and the purple glow brightened and swirled with the water. She wanted to cry out, but her uncle and father didn't seem to notice. Omid placed two coals on the grate and flashed his golden Zippo lighter from America.

As the flame neared the coals the purple glow began to throb and twist, dark violet into aborigine into electric lavender. As the flame began to lick the coals the whole hookah took on a metallic blue-violet tint.

"It's late Omid," said Farnoosh's father clapping the lighter shut and tossing it onto the table.

"I see. Your wife doesn't like my business, so my gifts aren't welcome here?"

"She doesn't want to be involved."

"Everyone is involved now. You might as well make the best of it. So the Shah stays and the English come in with their straws to drink up our oil. I'll sell them the straws. The Shah goes and this Imam I've been hearing so much about comes in. You can come and buy a bottle of cognac from me after mosque. There will always be rules and laws. That's just one persons idea of how the world should work. No one says they have to be real."

Ahmed looked at Farnoosh. Her eyes were glued to the water pipe. The rules had to be real for him.

"We'll smoke it another time, *inshallah*," he said. Omid looked dejected. Ahmed broke a comforting smile across his face. He had a way of calming anyone.

"We'll smoke next time. If it's still legal the next time we see each other," said Omid.

"Has the law ever stopped you from doing anything?"

"I know which laws to break and which to leave alone. That is why God takes care of me."

Omid turned on a heel and bent down to Farnoosh.

"I'll bring you another story, and maybe another Michael Jackson record," he said with a wink. He squeezed her cheek, chucked her chin, and left the hookah sitting on the coffee table.

Farnoosh's father gave her a smile with a touch of sadness and left the room, he ran his fingers along the hookah as he left the tearoom for his bedroom.

The hookah had a long brass stem that sunk into a blue water vase, made of intricately cut glass. The vase was like an azure diamond. The bowl of the hookah, packed full of tobacco was fashioned after an upturned right hand. Farnoosh recognized it as the "hamsa" or the hand of Fatima, an ancient symbol of safety and protection. She wore a necklace with a hamsa as long as she could remember; it had kept her relatively safe.

Then the power was cut. Curfew had come.

"Make sure the curtains are over the windows!" Farnoosh's mother called from the bedroom. Farnoosh obeyed, pulling the thick blackout curtains over the windows. She took one last peek outside. She imagined the Tuareg tent in the rolling sand dunes. She could hear helicopters in the distance, and the rumble of the army jeeps. These were details of the grown-up world that didn't require a twelve-year-old girl's opinion. Electricity was on sometimes and off sometimes, everyone had to be inside at night, except for Omid who according to him had very "good friends." She was left alone in the darkened room with the hookah and the bowl of sugar cubes.

Her eyes adjusted to the blackness of the room and she could make out the edges of the coffee table. She approached the bowl of sugar and put a cube on her tongue. She felt it submerge and dissolve in her mouth, but looking at the hookah sapped her mouth of all its saliva. She wanted to see the beautiful violet glowing like the lanterns in the bazaar. She placed her delicate fingers on coffee table, cool in the warm smoke-filled darkness. She slid her hands along the table until she found the golden Zippo lighter. It broke open easily in both of her hands and she thumbed the wheel. The olive skin of her face glowed like gold in the perfect darkness. She had tried her first cigarette months ago, and since she could remember was always fond of playing with fire.

Her fire-lit silhouette hovered in a pool of blackness. She picked up the mouthpiece to the hookah and wrapped her lips around it. The flame kissed the coal, air sucked through the stem, and water gurgled in the belly of the pipe as a blast of sweet smoke hit the back of her throat. She hoped the smell of her father's cigarettes would cover the aroma of the sweet shisha. As she inhaled the pulsating violet light bled out of the hookah and onto the floor forming a pool of deep purple light. Farnoosh choked on the smoke and doubled over into the carpet. She piled her hands on her mouth to keep herself from coughing. The violet form coalesced into a bare chested man in loose pants and slippers, with a ponytail jutting off of the top of his head. The man kneeled in supplication, his right hand held out, open palmed. A dull purple glow emanated from the man's skin, illuminating the room.

Farnoosh bit into her lip under her hands and tears filled in the corners of her eyes. Her parents would be furious if they found out she had smoked the hookah, and now there was a shirtless glowing man in their tearoom. The shirtless glowing man in their tearoom would equally enrage her parents.

The man said something in a language that she didn't understand. Their eyes met for the first time. They shared a confused silence then the man tried another language. And then another. She understood a word of what she recognized as English and then a couple of words of French, then Arabic. Spanish maybe? Perhaps Portuguese? And finally in Farsi the man said:

"Where am I?"

Farnoosh removed her hands from her mouth. She breathed out smoke from the hookah.

"Tehran. You're in Tehran," she whispered.

"You are my master now. You have three wishes."

Farnoosh jumped to her feet, ran up the stairs, piled all of the sheets on top of herself, and curled up into a ball around her favorite pillow.

She was in trouble.

Acknowledgements

So many people have given their time, effort, and guidance to this project. Immortal L.A. would not have happened without these people. I'm very blessed to have them in my life.

The Gibsons for being my second family. David Gibson for being there since second grade. Sara Perry, Deven Simonson for being my favorite artists to work with and my favorite people to drink with. Brittni Barger for being a passionate reader and a literary sorceress. Jenny Jensen for being the coolest godmother ever. Coffee Cartel for never changing and always having a power outlet free. Garrett Neimerg, Brenna Mickey, and Lauren Dukes for tolerating me for the last three years.

A very special thanks to Bruce Raterink, a champion of authors. This book would not be half of what it is without his tireless help, keen eye, and insane speed-reading. He an amazing human being that I am very fortunate to have met. A big thank you to Susan Merson, Jim Volz, and Evelyn Carol-Case. You've taught me every day since we met to lean in, listen up, be honest and work hard. I'm still trying my best. I think about you all every time I sit down to type.

I want to thank Joe Calarco for being a constant supporter of odd ideas and a great human. To all of the folks at Pseudopod who inspired the first story from this book and kept me company on many cold nights far from home.

A final thank you goes to Rebecca Forster, Josie Bates, Max the Dog, Archer, Hannah, and Billy – if it weren't for you guys I don't know where we would be.

About the Author

Eric Czuleger is from Los Angeles. He got a degree in acting from Cal State Fullerton. He came back to Los Angeles to be a founding member and resident playwright of Coeurage Theatre Company. He left Los Angeles again to be a Peace Corps Volunteer in Northern Albania. While overseas he wrote ten installments of "Live Theatre Blog" a monthly play about Albanian life that was performed in Hollywood and live streamed around the world. His other plays include, *Falling Dreams*, *Moonburn*, *Craigslist: Last Posts/Last Days*, *Head Over Heels*, *L.A. Lights Fire*, and *No. Saints Lane*.

Immortal L.A. is his first novel. Eric is currently working on his second novel **Farnoosh** as well as *Our Crowded Skies*: a live theatre documentary about UFO culture in America.

@Eczuleger

EricZuleger.com

eczuleger@gmail.com